JAMES DICKEY REVIEW

VOLUME 37

2021

JAMES DICKEY REVIEW

Editorial Staff
  Editor: William Walsh
  Managing Editor: Nikki Bowen
  Literary Editor: William Wright
  Researcher: Joel Langford
  Visual Design Consultant: Ashley S. Calicchia

  Assistant Editor: Jerry Rumph
  Copy Editor: Alicia Hughley
  Intern Reader: Althea Hughes
  Assistant Visual Design Consultant: Ariana "Avalon" Azahar
Social Media
  Facebook: James Dickey Review
  Twitter: @JamesDickeyRvw
Founding Editor
  Joyce M. Pair
Founding Editorial Board
  Matthew J. Bruccoli   Louis D. Rubin, Jr.
  Dave Smith   Monroe K. Spears
  Floyd C. Watkins, Jr.   Calhoun Winston
Advising Board Members
  Earl Braggs   Ward Briggs
  Richard Blanco   Denise Duhamel
  Gary Kerley   Donna Little
  Ellen Malphrus   Frank Paino
  Mark Roberts   Hugh Ruppersburg
  Gordon Van Ness   Megan Volpert
  Scott Wilkerson
Cover Design
  Ashley S. Calicchia
Cover Photograph
  Jerry Rumph

Editorial Policies

The *James Dickey Review* is published annually in December under the auspices of Reinhardt University's Etowah Valley MFA, a sixty-credit-hour, low-residency program (http://www.reinhardt.edu/MFA-CW/).

JDR publishes 1) scholarship that furthers the serious study of James Dickey's poetry, fiction, screenplays, and non-fiction (5,000 word limit; MLA style); 2) all forms of creative writing that align with Dickey's enduring themes, style, and literary experimentation (Fiction: 5,000 word limit; Non-fiction: 4,000 word limit; Poetry: not to exceeded five pages); 3) critical reflection essays by contemporary writers that analyze the creative process (2,000 word limit); 4) short reflections, meditations, and consideration on James Dickey, the man and the myth (1,000 word limit); 5) book reviews (500-750 word limit).

Send submissions in MS Word to *JamesDickeyReview@reinhardt.edu*. Reading period begins January 1 and ends June 1. Simultaneous submissions are welcome. Writers are notified of acceptance or rejection by September 1. Contributors are paid with one copy of the issue. Scholarly essays are accepted or rejected by JDR's Editorial Staff. Biographical essays, critical reflections, book reviews, and creative work are accepted or rejected by the Editorial Staff. Before submitting creative work, please be familiar with James Dickey's literary legacy and read *New Georgia Encyclopedia's* entry on James Dickey (http://www.georgiaencyclopedia.org/articles/arts-culture/james-dickey-1923-1997). Literary editors at *JDR* prefer creative writing that relies on vivid, sensory details and communicates the intensity of a real or imagined experience.

Purchasing and Subscription Information

James Dickey Review is published in print and in Kindle format by Amazon.com. Readers may purchase electronic and print copies at Amazon.com. Search for "James Dickey Review." Institutional & Library Subscriptions: $30; outside the U.S.: $30 + Shipping. Email inquiries to *JamesDickeyReview@reinhardt.edu*.

Postal Mail: *James Dickey Review*, c/o Bill Walsh, Etowah Valley MFA, Reinhardt University, 7300 Reinhardt Circle, Waleska, GA 30183
Electronic Mail: *JamesDickeyReview@reinhardt.edu*
Checks Payable: Reinhardt University
Indexing: The *James Dickey Review* is indexed by the MLA International Bibliography and Humanities Index International.

Contents

Editor's Preface

Since the *James Dickey Review* arrived on the Reinhardt University campus in 2015, this year may offer the biggest transition. Dr. Mark Roberts, who served as the editor for five years, became the President of the university this year, thus stepped down as editor. When asked to replace him, I gladly accepted the position. Having worked for four years as the literary editor, I did not foresee many changes; however, I felt there was a need for a new advisory board. I spent a few months carefully researching and then asking the right people to serve, which turned out to be those who have supported the journal for years, as well as others with new energy—scholars and creative writers. You might notice that several of the contributors in this issue are on the board. It's because they had already contributed or had ideas in the hopper when I asked them to serve. I am pleased with the level of professionalism of the advisory board, which holds to the standards set years ago— writers from all walks of life and literary styles and interests that create a balance between the scholarly and the creative.

As it does each year, the student editors change. The MFA program supplies the journal with bright, energetic students who work diligently to read and edit the best work submitted. The managing editor and the literary editor positions have also changed. From the outside looking in, a person might see nothing but upheaval; however, it's the antithesis. Everyone on the staff is united to focus on the goal, which is providing the best journal possible.

Among the material presented in this issue, we are fortunate to have four poems by Stephen Dunn, who a few years ago was a visiting writer at our summer residency. Within a few hours after the poems arrived, I accepted them for publication, but had heard from Stephen's daughter that he had been moved to hospice. Then four days later he died. It was a sad day because Stephen was one of my go-to poets for his work, specifically *Between Angels* (1989), which was an influential collection of poetry. I always thought he should have won the Pulitzer Prize for this volume, but it would be in 2001 for *Different Hours* that bestowed that honor. I met Stephen numerous times and considered him a friend. I once interviewed him for *Five Points* and drove him to the airport after his reading at Georgia Tech where we had a wonderful conversation in the car. There were a few times when he made suggestions to my poems. He was an athlete, but by the time I knew him, his health prevented him from playing tennis or one-on-one basketball. I could see it in his eyes that he wanted to take me on, and if he had been healthy, I'm certain he would have taken me down on the basketball court. He had been, after all, a pro basketball player. He was always a gentleman and had a great sense of humor. We are honored to offer his poems in this volume.

Two years ago, the university became the executors of George Scarbrough's creative work. Early in the year, Graham Foust emailed to ask for permission to reprint portions of a Scarbrough poem for an essay he had written. From that request came the idea for Foust to write on Scarbrough for the *JDR*. This year at the university, with a grant from CITEL, an unused room in the Lawson Building was converted into the George Scarbrough Center for Southern and Appalachian Literature, to house his life's work, personal papers, and mementos. It is a museum-quality room that also serves as the home of the *James Dickey Review* and *Sanctuary*, the university's undergraduate literary journal.

The *JDR* is moving forward with thoughts and ideas on James Dickey's work, but also creative pieces and scholarly articles on other subjects. The editors and advisory board believe this is a formidable balance for the academic and educated generalist, and we hope everyone enjoys what is presented.

William Walsh

POETRY

A Handmaid's Incantation Against Silence

In the names of The Mothers I go forth
in the likeness of a child, in the likeness of a bud,
in the likeness of a stone fort,
in the likeness of a deer coming to a river's split
and stronger I am than each,

and wiser I am than he
who named himself The Master,
he who wept when I swayed to an island song,
he who turned my silk purse inside out,
he who tore skirts like feathers from my closet,
he who threatened red petals at my door,
he who found the claims outrageous,
he who held a hand upon my hip
and pulled me in towards him
like a dog pulling a bone out of the dirt.
Come now, you know how it is.
    (Come now, I know how it is!)

May I be all lark rising against the iron sky.
May I be nine blades of yarrow beneath a right heel
and the tenth as a tithe to the elders of the bog.

Yarrow is to wound what light is to house.
Yarrow is the end of *not this, not this, not this.*
Yarrow is the hand of seven cures.
Yarrow is a tongue set loose.

Annemarie Ní Churreáin

The Daughter Who Went Missing

If I were to tell you that a vigil was held —
candles lit, prayers said —

or that long beams of silver torchlight scanned
the village in search,

or that the river-bailiff soaked by rain was forced
to plead with the villagers,
Somebody must know something

I would be lying.

Quietly, darkness fell
upon railway tracks, outhouses, derelict sheds,
upon an empty nest curled into a leafless oak,
upon a foothold trap shimmering in the forest
like a buried star,

as all night the river kept rising,
the mess at the end unstirred

and outside the house of the missing girl
a black raven cawed,
Traitors, traitors, traitors.

Annemarie Ní Churreáin

The Screaming Room

*At the Mother and Baby Home, Castlepollard, County
Westmeath (1935-1971)*

Shoulder against the outhouse door,
I push until light gives way to half-light
and find on the other side a roof caved-in,
a mud floor tangled in bramble, an empty dresser
toppled over like a ship in the ocean's gut.
It reeks in here of the secrets of the earth.
Did these walls conceal the sound an infant
made of the body as it travelled down
along darkness into the unholy strangeness
of its own new life? Were the girls told to breathe
as they opened? Were those breaths counted
with the same precision as other fortunes?
And later, when the birth cry hit the clean,
bleached air, did anyone declare beauty?
I come from women who found themselves
in trouble, who turned to their pale reflections
and asked, *What can I do? What can I do?*
All that fire, all that burning. In their honour
I can never again be silent.

Annemarie Ní Churreáin

A Charm to Protect a Girlchild

Be patient. Wait by a window.
You want a robin, but not inside
the house. It is enough to look
through glass. *There he is. There he is.*
Little bond-bird, guardian of news.
The robin unpicks earth's prophecies,
thorn by thorn, feathers the world
in breath, heals the blood-path
with moss and leaf. Let him be
a sign of *spheres to come*. Rid yourself
of lock and key. Go closer to the flame.
Once the elders carved out of this
tiny breast the heart-stone and wore it
for luck. The robin knows death,
but is not death. In the omen tongue
the girl who cannot be stolen
is named *spideog*. Speak the language
of the robin. Become apprentice
to snow. Chant *life, greater
than crucifixion.*

Annemarie Ní Churreáin

The Taming of The Shrew

Faith, as you say, there's small choice in rotten apples.
—Hortensio to Grumio, I, i

Can we forgive the one who murders, who
betrays? Does motive matter? Circumstance?
Hunger? Beating scars? Being named a shrew?

Doug Pastorchik was poor—his house, one glance
told me when we wandered in from playing,
a dirty my mother would not allow.

Doug's older brother—thirteen to our nine?—
gave me my first sight of a cig pack rolled
in a T-shirt sleeve, eyed me a small sign
I take now to have meant embarrassment,
took then as threat or sneer, an instant grasping
tight my fear. We could not break the distance frame.

There was dogshit on the rug. I can't recall his name.

Stephen Corey

The Histories of Your Past and Future: Lesson 1

The past had a past it was trying to overcome,
one about which it believed improvements had been made;
the future looks back your way with amazement, hatred,
berating your arrogance, your dumb and fumbling ways.

Stephen Corey

Shylock and Romeo, the Only Two . . .

. . . who have left the stage and entered the world
via dictionary definition,
whose huge energies of greed and passion
earned them front-row dictionary places,
their names no longer names nor instances
but—trochaic, dactylic—the bare, forked
things themselves. Be not a Shylock. Perhaps
be not a Romeo—"philanderer"
no, but "ardent lover" yes—yet these two
are one as well as two, while a Shylock's
a Shylock only: bloodthirsty, fated
to a bottommost circle, yet famous.

Stephen Corey

For You at My Death

Either way, I could not do this then:

I'll be the one to sign off first,
joining the great dumb legions of Houdinis
swearing they would offer a sign,

or you will have gone, cutting me short
in the way of that great wooden crate
dropping from its corner perch
in the Tew Street garage—I was, what,
seven or eight?—to seal me flat beneath,
its vacuum leaving me with the first-ever breath
I could not take, even now those stymied lungs
a bright terror, though only seconds passed
before playmates lifted it to set me free.

Oh, but there would be no lifting,
only stones on the chests of poets
everywhere, the day you passed
and I was left behind to . . .

Stephen Corey

Damage

My mother was careful not to fall,
chose each step as deliberately
as she chose her words, each one
straightened in place like her half-slip.

I thought of her before dawn
when I walked up my narrow stairs
in the dark holding my coffee and a stack
of books. I almost tripped, remembered

how careful she was, would never put
herself in jeopardy, didn't want an injury,
would never carry a high stack of books
and coffee filled to the brim

up a narrow staircase in the dark, but this
is how we're different. I can be reckless,
impulsive, spurt out, fall in love, ruin a day
with one wrong step, drop a platter of cold cuts

onto the wet grass seconds before presenting
to my guests, can fall off the roof of a sidewalk,
back into the side of a truck, let a word slide
out of my mouth like a rusty razor blade,

let myself fall for the impossible. Oh the puddles
I've stepped in, the hairs I've allowed to go
down the drain, the parts of myself I've swept
to the curb, some still moving.

Kim Dower

Save Barbie

The father in the pool at the tennis club
is playing "Rescue" with his three-year-old.
He tosses her naked Barbie into the deep end
so his daughter will feel compelled to jump
in and rescue her. SAVE BARBIE he yells.
She doesn't want to do this. She doesn't care
if Barbie drowns. This is the father's way
of teaching his daughter to swim. He assumes
his toddler is desperate to save the doll, but
her crossed arms say she doesn't care if Barbie
lives or dies. This surprises the father who throws
the doll again and again, each time yelling SAVE
BARBIE to the terrified child by the edge of the pool.
Someone needs to tell Dad this is not a great game.
Now I hear him telling her that he's a shark
and unless she can dive in and grab Barbie, the shark
will eat her. I am hoping this happens. I would love to see
this man force Barbie down his throat. I may, in fact,
do it for him. I can assure you that as much as I loved my Barbie,
I would have been fine seeing her drown or eaten by a shark.
I'd never fall for a dumb game like this. I had a real
swimming teacher, one with a whistle dangling from her neck,
a red cross bathing suit, one who taught me how to breathe
from my diaphragm.

Kim Dower

Doing Nothing

I lie down on my bed, pretend to read
On the Road, the book I always lie about
having read. I stare out the window,
think about the day Miss Josephs,
my fifth grade teacher, shared my book report
on *The Red Pony* with the class:
an example of really excellent work!
But today I'm doing nothing, just staring
at my fingernails. I choose to believe
the latest research, that doing nothing can lead
to bursts of creativity, ideas flowing
like a revitalized creek through a ghost town.
Lava can erupt from an inactive volcano.
I get up from the bed and sit on the floor
in a half spinal twist, apologize to the dead,
which takes a few hours since many people I love
have recently died. *I'm sorry I didn't come over sooner,*
I tell my mother; *sorry, Dad, I made fun of you*
when you said things like "he's as old as the hills."
I'm sorry to a poet who loved me.
To be precise, and completely fair to myself,
the word "doing" in front of the word "nothing" changes
the word nothing—lifts it into the world of action.
I realize this as I stare at the electrical outlet,
wonder what I should plug into it,
what kind of lamp might work well in that corner.
Maybe one of those tall skinny metal poles,
three bulbs shooting straight up —
something to illuminate the ceiling, but no,
it'll look cheap, out of style, and anyway,
maybe I should keep one part of the room dark,
so ideas might grow like mushrooms, populate

my brain with plans I won't pursue.
It might be time to *really* read *On the Road*,
but another's stream of consciousness
competing with my own might incite an inertia tsunami.
I'm sorry to the dogs I loved but never cleaned up after.
I'm sorry for all the time I wasted as a child,
when doing nothing was all they expected of the girl
with the chalkboard and dolls.

Kim Dower

The Prayer You Asked For

For Carolyn, my sister-in-law

When I asked what you wanted for Christmas,
you said you wanted a prayer from me
sincere, unironic, because you were
about to have surgery, and needed one.

I hereby pray that all goes well, and you heal
speedily and fully, and that the God
you believe in, a God of beneficence
and salvation, is listening.

Because you know I've long maintained
that to pray is to address a better part
of oneself, I want you to trust
that belief doesn't matter to me now,

only love does in this grand unruly scheme
of our lives together. And if there is
a celestial being, a possibility
for your sake I'll allow myself to imagine,

let Him descend as quietly and as invisibly
as ever. The only proof I want is your health,
some proper restoration of your body,
this Christmas and for years to come. Amen.

Stephen Dunn

In the Battle Against Tyranny

In the battle against tyranny
be prepared to lose a skirmish
or two. Maybe even more.
We need to know those in power
never forget people like us
have a score to settle, remain
galvanized by grief and rage.
They hire henchmen
so they can take naps
in the afternoon, and offset
the worry of enemies skulking
on the outskirts
of their enormous properties.
They want to be free to dream
of winding tunnels and fortified
stairways leading to places
where they can't be found.
But we the aggrieved always
have a sense of where they are.
It may take years before we find
the words that turn into a plan.

That's when we have to keep
hitting them hard above the belt.
Even after they catch on,
they're often fooled by tactics
not theirs. Remember
we have language now.
We can use it like a shield
to protect us
or to confuse them
with pretty stories
of ascensions into the clouds,
the ones in which kings
try to become gods, and discover
how sad it can be to succeed.

Stephen Dunn

During the Pandemic

Many claimed for themselves
an understandable loneliness,
though for some it was a continuation
of a way of being, habitual,
tiresome, hard to befriend.

In the evenings, less lonely
by luck or temperament,
I'd wet my soul
with wine, try to legitimize

who I was by vowing
not to nod to nonsense.
I was used to filling my life
with good cheer and the little
thrills of invention,

yet I heard how many lies
kept being repeated until
they sounded like the truth.
People were dying
and getting shot in the back

and knelt upon
until breathless. Suddenly
alone like never before
with the feelings of others
I understood

part of being excluded
is the need to claim as yours
everything
you can't expect
anyone will ever give you

Stephen Dunn

Love Poem Near the End of the World

This is the world I'm tethered to:
clouds, lavender-tinged, and below them
russet-going-on-green hillsides.
Everywhere various aspirations
of transcendence, like my fickle heart
wishing to redefine itself
as an instrument of hope and generosity,
and flower beds
with just enough rainwater
to turn cracked soil into a vast blossoming.
Something keeps me holding on
to a future I didn't think possible.
There's sweetness and there's squalor.

There are sad, almost empty towns
occasionally brightened by fireworks.
And there's you, my love, once volcanic,
beautifully quiet now.

Stephen Dunn

Adagio

As to the rain, we sleep best
when it comes and comes,
hard or soft but fully
lost in its own performance,
keeping us still. The deep
furrows we have fallen into
with merci. Oh, my philosopher
of the fanfare. Oh, my mistress of the cello.
Not a peep
all night long. Underneath,
however, how clear, how beautifully
alert we turn out, joining hands
to face solving for x
in the morning's music.

Gary Gildner

Scherzo

After surfacing
inside the pool of early
morning mountain air
washing wild fragrance
over the lotion of romance,
I see the river make its bracelet-
bright way among the boulders
down the valley, hear the wind
(blowing just right) broadcast
horny rams smacking heads
for dibs on the juicy ewes
waiting, chewing sideways;
and dancing round and round
with a feather pen
behind my ear
—a regular Faunus
tooting his flute, pulling off
an old soft-shoe the old hoofer
almost forgot.

Gary Gildner

Somewhere Outside the Hall of Fame

Pull over at the next stop, you say
and I do, but the exit is only
an overpass, an off-ramp sloping up
through an hour of oak and maple
in each direction, hills of fields
and a few farms, not a sign
of the nearest town, so I park
on the shoulder, and you shuffle
past the reach of the headlights
to piss in a roadside bush,
the shadow of you as real
as your real figure fading
in the evening light, and though
we never said it, both of us knew
that the still-green leaves left
on those trees would be spectacular
in the fall, a blaze of gold and cardinal,
but we wouldn't be there to see it.

Timothy Green

Ötzi

*Ötzi is the natural mummy of a man who lived between
3400 and 3100 BCE, discovered in 1991 in the Ötztal Alps*

You've made a museum of me.
Stacked stones like blue ice
at the feet of my mountain.

We pile our stones on the peaks
where the wind speaks in the voices
of the gods. Am I one of your gods?

Is this why you brought me here?
I whisper but there is no wind.
Your torchlights never flicker

in this smooth room. Everything
echoes. What would you like
to know? The secrets of time?

What is time but the spine
of a mountain bending back?
And what is a story but the arc

of time? You know mine.
You've made a map of my meals.
You've measured my wounds

with every kind metal. I worked
with metal; I know the rocks
that weep and the power of a blade.

But I'll tell you what you know:
I climbed down to the village
and the smoking huts were

too much smoke. I killed two
painted men with the same arrow.
Wrestled with a knife and fled.

They found me by my fire
two days later, my belly full of meat
and bread. You found me, still full

of that meat and bread. I'll tell you
what you really want to know:
Was I happy in my primitive life?

Was I happier than you are now?
Yes. So happy that I fled.
So happy that I built the flame

and ate the bread that brought
the arrow I knew was coming.
So happy with life that the ice

was all I had left to turn to.

Timothy Green

SWEET POTATO

The 1997 census shows that Black farmers owned 1.5 million acres of "farmable land," down from 16-19 million acres in 1910.

1

Food travels, the speaker said.

These came over that Mason Dixie:
stewed tomatoes, green tomatoes, fried corn,
fried pies, grits, sawmill gravy, okra,
parched peanuts, field peas, sweet potato pie,
fried sweet potatoes, baked sweet potatoes,
and candied sweet potatoes.

I am Black. I am black-eyed peas.
I am the blackened, scorched peel of a sweet potato,
the potato left roasting on a stone hearth
(Lillian did this), hot coals and ash mounded
over orange tubers: old way, old ways
and dark bodies heading to the fields in darkness.
Dawn coming, the sky is blackberry juice
and hearth-roasted sweet potatoes.

2   After the West African Folktale

Once a woman wanted a child.
She planted a sweet potato slip
beside her hut. It grew into a child.

The Sweet Potato Child swept, and
scrubbed, and cooked. She did all
that daughters do. But a child is a child.

The woman scolded, "You are nothing
but lump and leaf I dug from dirt!"

The Sweet Potato Child left and stood
in the dirt beside her mother's hut.
Her hair twisted into vines.
Her arms and legs grew long, long, long
and bent crooked into roots.

The woman wailed and struggled to pull
her daughter from the dirt.
The Sweet Potato Child sank.
The woman pulled with both hands.
The Sweet Potato Child sank.

The sinking took a long time.

I told you it took a long time.

Did you listen?

3

Listen—they sold all that land.
Nobody was going back there.
Least they got something for it. Can't blame 'em.
These young people don't care nothing.

At Tuskegee, Carver made vinegar, molasses,
postage stamp glue, synthetic rubber, and ink
from sweet potatoes.

Have you ever sipped sweet potato wine
or brewed it in a five-gallon jug?

It's not just the slow charring that sweetens, but
more the ash, even more the chop-chop of Lillian's hoe,
the slurry of horse manure ladled from a bucket.
Say there was nothin' she couldn't grow. Had two gardens.
What they had to live off of. That woman worked all the time.

A sweet potato needled with toothpicks
grows in a mason jar filled with tap water
atop my kitchen counter.

Fewer than 2% of all United States farmers
are African American. How many grow sweet potatoes?

4

In the evening, after supper
she pared a sweet potato. She peeled the skin
and scraped her blade against the orange meat.
She lifted a mince of pulp and brought it by knife edge,
a coarse confection, to a child's lips.

The child's tongue, mothy-greedy, fluttered,
and beat for more.

The child chewed and swallowed,
consumed the potato.

But the sweetness stayed, and the child,
bearing its ink upon her tongue,
wrote her first words.

Cover your words with ash.
Leave them to sear, blacken.

Paradox: it's the heat, the burning,
that draws the sweetness.

Janice N. Harrington

GOLDFISH

Hearing the stutter of our heels against the brick,
or seeing our shadows slanted over the pond's lip,
the fish rise—Koi and catfish—to lip and suck
the doughy pellets, the boon spilled from cupped palms.

Fish and the shadows of fish settle beside stems
of cattails, settle in the rooted shade of water lilies
and hyacinths, their delicate fins signing proofs
of buoyancy and equations of depth.

We slip—daughter and daughter's child,
—slip beneath the waters of the pond
and rise again under older waters, under the rim
of another pond shaped with concrete and cinderblocks,
its oak-stained waters filled with lilies
and tadpoles, with shying goldfish and fractures of light,
the pond that Websta built long ago, dredging
its sand and yellow clay into wheelbarrows,
and wrenching well water and the store
of rain barrels to sate its emptiness.

From the shadows of that older pond, we see
Webster sitting splay-legged on a wooden bench,
heels pushed into the sand, drawing fins of smoke
into his nostrils from a hand-rolled cigarette. This ritual,
after chores, when the heat is high: to sit beside
the pond under the eaves of a pin oak and watch,
for the length of a cigarette, clouds and water lilies
clotted in the brownblack water of a goldfish pond.

Yet what came to him out of the smoke and still water?
Out of the unseen undulations of goldfish?
Out of water lilies or the mania of dragonflies?
To a man whose hems were shat with pasture mud,
whose hard hands were cured by work?

Sounding, we listen as fish do. We listen but do not
call his name, do not slap our spines against the water
to draw his eye. He does not see us or suspect fish that bear
the faces of a woman or a distant child or think
that beneath his floating world are past and future
and future pasts, that all the waters are joined.
It is only a pond he sits beside, a pond he built himself.
If the heifer bawls, he will answer. After the heat's traces lift
from his body, he will rise from his slow considerations.
When the cigarette is ash, he will grind it with a hard heel
and walk away. We hear, for a long while, as fish do,
his steps against the sand, but we cannot stay. Turning,
we sink again, under the long-rooted waterlilies, rising
once more. *Come with me*, she says, *help me feed the fish.*

Janice N. Harrington

BODIES

The Golden Age fire, 11-22-1963
The Kennedy assassination, 11-22-1963

Soot, cinders, tethered to a blackened-rail,
a woman's hand and wrist, charred bones,
     they remove all that's left,
the coal-black, man-shaped chunk, and inside
the fever-colored meat. They carry it away.

"Let them see what they have done."

Blood-stained, flesh-spattered. She would not take it off.
Only afterwards, after the plane landed, after they removed
his casket from the plane. Let them see.

Black smoke, black smolder.
Insatiable, the flame wanted more, to hold,
to fondle everything. It wanted to press its skin
against their geometries, to press, as a lover would,
their softer forms.

       Black sear, black scald.
The flame opened its mouth: to taste,
to lick, to bite, bite, bite. The flame spat nothing out.

Sunny. Unseasonably warm. Crowds and placards.
Cheers, glad-shouts, a crack of air.

His body slumped against her shoulder. A moment
before: a spray, the bright blossom from his head.

———————————

The flames grew, unfurling like buds, stems,
leaves, blossoms.

Then the fruit—old men and old women—
their swelling vowels, the ripe syllables of their screams.

Passersby rushing toward the flames.

———————————

"I . . . saw . . . a bundle of pink, just like a drift

of blossoms, lying on the back seat."

Her body lay across his.

———————————

Some made it out, then turned and went in again.
They hid in the shower, under beds,
in a closet, but the flames found them.
A 90-year-old forgot her purse—she went back.

———————————

"Let them see what they have done."

———————————

Fire fighters, volunteers, coroners
stepping amidst the ruins, searching,
wrenching aside bedsprings, the metal frame of a wheelchair.
The stench melded into their nostrils: burnt meat.

———————————

November 22, 1963.

Banner headline: Dallas

(The largest nursing home fire in history, page 10.)

Everyone remembers where they were.

———————————

In Ohio, near Fitchville, 21 coffins beside a mass grave.

———————————

It was the color: strawberry-pink.

The suit he chose for her, rough boucle, navy collar, navy piping
on each sleeve and pocket, six buttons. Not Chanel, or haute couture,
only a copy, like so many things a replication, even history.
Her husband said she looked ravishing.

Janice N. Harrington

THE ART OF SCALDING

After washing the dishes to scald them,
boiling water to ward fever and croup,
after glands *swoll as big as chicken eggs,*
or *trying to keep us from coming down with it,*

after rising steam and scourging heat—always
this final act—ablution, a bond to secure
those she loved, hot water sploshed
on melamine and mason jars, scarred skillets
and *butcha* knives, her ritual, her psalm:
water surged from a kettle's spout.

Once, I spilled a saucepan of boiling water
on Anna's thigh. She wept, and quick-quick
she soothed the blistered flesh with vinegar
and baking soda, and then with ice. Neither
cursing, nor scolding, nor rage. Neither
tongue nor hand lifted to strike or bruise.

How terrible forgiveness. How it sears and scalds.
I would rather she screamed, *Look what you did!*
I would rather she shouted, *You stupid, clumsy girl!*

Janice N. Harrington

HALLOW

> *Thou shalt write them on the posts*
> *of thy house and on thy gates.*
> *Deuteronomy 6:9*

On Lillian's porch, this small sanctuary:
wash basins, coffee tins, and sauce pans
potted with petunias, impatiens,
rock roses, and widow's tears,
a mess of homey flowers, as Hurston wrote.

Vines and sunlight on lips of graniteware.
Rust-rotted, dinted, but still
they do their work: hold soil and roots,
bright petalled fastenings and binding vines.

Draw the eye to and toward and from.
Well, I best be getting on . . . And this redress,
that she had troubled that leaving and loss,
delayed the silence, at least for a little while.

Janice N. Harrington

Barbershop Legends

Come sit down, youngblood
And hold real still
While I cut your head
And tell you tales
Of the last of the barbershop legends
The best ballers
You've never heard of
Who never made it
Past that imaginary county line
Who once could run circles around defenders
Until smoke took their lungs
Who once could handle the rock like an extension of their limbs
Until drugs caused their hands to shake, nerves to wane
Who once could pick coins off the rim in a single jump
Until diabetes took their legs
Sugar and fat redoubling their weight upon this earth
Who once could run these courts care free, pickup games every weekend
Until lust gave them children to ignore, women to escape, alimony to pay
Their sneakers long since traded for liquor bottles
Or worse
Oh they could have gone pro
Just ask them
You can find them all around
That one boy still has the high school record for most points
The number burned into a plaque high in the trophy case
But he cannot read it from his cell, upstate, doing 8 years for armed robbery
Was it the Johnson kid who had a scholarship waiting?
His education in trade for putting that ball through the hoop
He left the papers unsigned on the table
Took a job with his uncle fixing cars
Has a hoop over the loading bay he cannot look at without crying

Remember that boy who could dunk in junior high?
Yonder on the wall is a newspaper with him on the front page
Died of drugs that same year at season's end
That picture you see is the last basket he would ever make
Where have they all gone
These hometown legends
Now blacktop kings
Proudly telling the world who they were
Struggling to hide from what they are
Searching for what is left
There now, your hair is done
You rise in long shorts, a stained jersey
Shoes half a size too big
But you will grow
Are still growing into a man
Your moves may come, youngblood
Perhaps even glory
But they will fade with one ill decision
So steeped in finality
Go live your life well
And I will pray
That I never see that head again
To cut in the darkness of this single chair
Surrounded by framed ghosts on the walls that taunt us
And the broken husks of men in chairs waiting their turn
Quick to remind us they are
The last of the barbershop legends

Kincaid Jenkins

Applause

Because our fingertips sound
of loosening bones,
        not willingly,

toward the earth. In these palms,
an encounter, a wordless signal

        to describe a hunt or to praise
                some ancient fire.

And the mind
remembers the past in the sound

of absence:

no banging,
        no clicking,
                no vowels

just nerve endings to each other
whispers of what happened.

Daniel Lassell

Exodus

I walk with my lover to floodplains
down past highway 23, rubble and weeds,
and the rail systems rusted near the dog pound.
We can hear them barking.

I say I'm glad to be living,
satisfied with fields this autumn, as the school year
passes over in its deadlines. And we're okay.
We watch a dog bound through clicking wheat stalks

to a deer with a flicked tail, running
headlong into woods. We look around
at our happiness. Even though this town
crawls over itself; even though

the years are like the jobs, shadows
in tandem with our neighbors, all of us
wading into a wind thick with worried income,
into the future we've never trusted.

Yet, if this place could speak,
if far-off barn walls could lean into us,
I'm sure they'd ask, *Don't you see
what's growing from your heads?*

Silence stirs in the wild of any wild thing,
deep recesses of wanting—and of not.
Gratitude: the absence of want.
And yet, don't we all want gratitude?

Today I walk with my lover,
her hand softly in mine—and that's enough
for today, to have this moment
and the quiet turning of sky.

Daniel Lassell

Visitant

for James Dickey

In the sun-heightened quiet
that follows summer rain
you appear
at the kitchen window

and as you speak
you rest your fingers
on the wet mesh.

I raise mine
to meet them
and where they touch
droplets run in
lines like bars—
but I already know
you won't be staying for supper.

Through that flutter of the veil
I see
there is no end to deliverance—

yet even after you fade
I cannot take my hand
from the screen.

Ellen Malphrus

Earth

The earth is up to it again,
Rotating into darkness
No memory of daylight

The sea opens its mouth
Waves crash on the shore...

Darkness is always slippery
Daylight, solid
The heart knows the boundaries of both

There is always another side to things
Sometimes we belong to each
Not sure what direction to take

Everyone is wet and cold
Dryness will not happen without a towel
Sometimes, you have to approach things differently
Fall in love with the edge

Gloria Mindock

Surface

Daylight decodes this moment.
It is the Holy Grail for life.

There is nothingness, silence,
restlessness, dark fighting for control.

My heart dances, stops.
Dances, dreams.
Dances, spins.

Whatever is to come
will be delivered
spinning into certainty

I use to think that I felt
I was wrong

coldness like steel, there is
no breaking.
My surface is forming a barrier
where I flourish in the void.

Gloria Mindock

Batting Practice

My cousins' coach picked us up at the farm
in an old Ford Fairlane station wagon
gutted and raggedy, rattling like a boxcar
and we drove deep into the bottoms on
narrow ancient black-tar country roads
till we came to a tarpaper shack sunken
into a hackberry thicket and from it emerged
two boys, brothers, thirteen and fourteen
years old but big as men and shaped
by work as if they'd been driving railroad
spikes with sledgehammers, and they got in
with us, filled up the rest of the old car,
and we drove back out of the bottomland
to a ballfield, one corner of somebody's
pasture off the highway and watched them
knock the snot out of some baseballs.
I don't remember what happened after that,
or what became of those two quiet fellows,
or if they still live down there in the bottoms,
or of the coach and his rusting-out Fairlane,
or even one of my two cousins, disappeared
from our lives years ago. The coach pitched
batting practice from the homemade mound
with a gentle smile on his face, and the balls,
when they smacked them, arced toward the sun,
as it was sinking in the west, like meteors
traveling off into the immensity of space.

Nick Norwood

The Road to Macon

Most houses along that stretch between Salem
and Lizella are small wood-frames. Rural, their
owners set out flowers and shrubs and paint their
siding colors you won't see in town. The road

is narrow, gently winding, drops down to cross
creek bottoms, then climbs slowly back. I love
the moment in late winter when the roadside
thicket looks snarled and tangled as the wiring

harness out of one of those old radios whose
sound, when they worked, was pure and sweet
heard through the whir of a black steel tabletop
fan in somebody's country kitchen. And then

the redbuds and dogwoods pop like an unexpected flashing in the heart that warms
and glows and slowly fades against the gray-
brown wiring of that ancient machine, and sitting

outside in old metal lawn chairs painted lime
green, royal blue, carmine, canary, the country
folks, waving nonchalantly as you pass, are already turning back to their conversations.

Nick Norwood

FICTION

Caritas

On the 80th floor, men in three-thousand-dollar suits and silk shirts filled the boardroom of Global Technologies, debating the legal minutiae of an acquisition agreement. They argued about the conditions under which the smaller, more vulnerable International Industries would bend to Global Tech's strategy of acquisition. The board of I.I. had been ambushed with a letter of intent by Global two months prior to this meeting. It was a classic M&A maneuver, a "hostile takeover," calculated, bloodless, but no less grisly. A quarter till nine, the representatives of both companies were in the middle of fierce negotiation. Razor-sharp words of barb-wired legal jargon— termination rights, covenants, and provisions—sliced through objections as useless as tissue paper. Harvard lawyers and Columbia MBAs fought it out in a bare-knuckle cage match, thinly disguised as a cordial discussion of asset divisions, leadership restructuring, and workforce consolidation. They brawled over the terms of a reconceived joint company, crafting the language to maximize future profits for Global Tech and their shareholders. International Industries, their flailing prey, gasped for air.

Frank Harrison, CEO of Global, coordinated the attack, working to outflank, outthink, and outwit Sam Neville, his counterpart at the target company. Frank was smart, ambitious, and unconstrained by ethics. Sam was no less savvy, but this melee was fundamentally unsettling and he was doing all he could to protect himself and salvage something of the company he had built. It was a grim struggle for so early in the morning. But it was just business, the type of complicated, vicious transaction that happened every day in Manhattan.

A minute later, everything changed forever.

The fuel-filled wings of the Boeing 767 were sheared off on impact, driving the fuselage into the center of the building in an explosive blast. Out of the fireball erupted a massive cloud of smoke. The plane had not carried a bomb. It was, in itself, a targeted incendiary device. The jet fuel burned hot and fast, swallowing mass in an instant, melting steel like wax, liquefying concrete. The aircraft crumpled and detonated several floors of offices. The executives and members of the boards of these two companies felt the violent shudder in the frame of the building. Thick, acrid smoke began to fill the hallways, curling into rooms, billowing among cubicles. Although the flames had not licked their way onto the 80th floor yet, the heat, vapor, and sickening lurch of floors, walls, and equipment had turned the Global Tech headquarters into a terrifying warzone. Overhead lights flickered, ceiling panels dropped, fire alarms wailed. Civilized order exploded into savage entropy.

The blast knocked Sam out of his chair and slammed his head on the corner of the century-old oak table that dominated the boardroom. He dropped, unconscious, onto the plush crimson carpet beside his chair. As people scrambled to find their way out of the room, lost in the dark, screaming in panic, hacking in the smoke, running into scattered furniture, Sam was serene in the contracted world contained in his skull. No one saw him where he lay. Sixty seconds before, there was grand talk about corporate solidarity and company loyalty and strategic cooperation. Now it was every man and woman for themselves.

The half-conscious ones were blinded by the particles saturating the atmosphere and clouding their vision. Shielding their eyes with one hand and covering their mouths with the other, they stumbled like drugged lab rats in a maze. Sam's lungs struggled to pull in and expel the thick air. A normally gracious female board member stumbled over him, kicking his shoulder on her way out the door. His brainstem kept him breathing, his blood circulating, as memories projected in his brain's mysterious nexus of mass and mind.

"Samuel?" his mother shouted from the back porch. "Where are you? It's time for dinner! Find your sister and wash up!"

He was floating in his best friend's swimming pool, resting on a plastic inflatable raft. The sun was slowly baking his tender body, but he was happy, happy in a way an adult can never quite duplicate. He had no class assignments to worry him. He had done his chores for the week and the requests for lawn mowings had not yet come in. Sam didn't have a care in the world. He was young and warm, resting atop the cool water, the canopy of clear blue sky above him, unmarred by clouds.

"Samuel?" his mother shouted again, wiping her hands on her apron.

"Hey, Sam," his friend mumbled from an adjacent float. "I think your momma wants you to come home."

"Huh?" he replied lazily.

"Time to call it a day, buddy."

"Mmmm."

"Hey," his friend said more insistently, splashing a handful of water in Sam's direction. "We can do this again tomorrow. Time for some grub now."

"Okay, okay," Sam said, slowly paddling to the edge of the pool and then easing onto the pavement.

He toweled off and nodded to his friend, "Thanks for another awesome day. See you tomorrow." He turned to leave, then said over his shoulder, "Maybe something different. The mall?"

"Maybe," was the reply. "See ya."

"Yeah, later."

It was a short walk to his house, less than a block. His towel was wrapped over his head like a monk's cowl, shielding him from the late afternoon sun. He didn't see the kid blocking the sidewalk until he ran into him.

"What the…?" he sputtered, stumbling back.

"Well, if it isn't little Sammy Neville, neighborhood sissy and all-around weenie," the bigger boy barked down at him.

Sam tensed but said nothing for a moment. He assessed, as he always did, what his chances were in a fight with this kid. The other boy was big but slow. Sam was quick but didn't have the developed muscles of his adversary.

"What's up, Frank?"

"That's Mr. Harrison to you, punk," the big kid said.

No response.

"Have you forgotten our arrangement?" Frank asked. "Every time you see me, you owe me a dollar."

Sam glared at him.

"Don't have a dollar," Sam said, pulling at his swim trunks.

"Then next time you owe me two, loser," Frank spat, punching him in the gut.

Sam doubled over and hobbled home, wheezing.

"Jesus said to 'Love thy enemies,' Samuel," his mother would remind him. "But that doesn't mean you can't stand up for yourself, son."

He slinked up to his room and shut the door. He was running out of money.

Seventeen minutes later, United Airlines Flight 175 hit the South Tower. Sam was still out, wandering among the library of scenes that congealed to form his history. For him, time had ceased its forward motion. The kinetic activity, the profound disorder, the terrifying convulsion of metal and flame and flesh was unknown to him. He saw only the unspooling of his own story in the cinema of his mind.

"So we were sitting in English class," Sam was telling his friend, his mouth locked in an enormous grin, "and I looked over, and guess who was staring at me?"

"I don't know."

"Sandy," Sam said. "It was Sandy. Gorgeous, brilliant, adorable Sandy. Looking at me. Then she passes a note up to me. And guess what?"

"What?"

"She wants to go out."

Pause.

"Out. Yeah, out. Like to a movie or something."

"You gonna ask her?"

"What kind of idiot would I be if I didn't? I mean, she is the most—"

Someone slammed Sam up against the locker. His friend backed away from the giant standing there, wearing a football letter jacket.

"So, Sammy, when are you going to get me the answers to the geometry homework?" Frank said, leaning in, nose to nose with Sam.

"I, um, I don't have it," he said.

"Did I just hear you say you don't have what I need?" Frank's hand balled into a fist. "I thought we had an understanding."

"And I'm not going to get it," Sam said, softly but firmly.

"What?" the linebacker asked, color rising in his cheeks.

"I said, 'You can do your own damn homework.'"

There was a span of darkness before Sam woke up in the nurse's clinic. With a bloodied nose, bruised ribs, and a couple of aspirins, he was discharged and routed to the principal's office. A stern lecture, a warning, and then he was sent home.

"Jesus said to 'Pray for those who persecute you,' Samuel," his mother said, once he walked in the back door and she had determined that he was battered but essentially in one piece. "But he didn't say you had to put up with bullies. I'm proud of you, son. I don't like you fighting, but I'm glad you're not letting that boy push you around."

He went to bed with an extra serving of custard that night.

His thoughts were flashing more quickly, jumbled, frantic. He slipped into awareness as noise and fumes spilled into his pristine memories. He started to gag and cough and then he was no longer a teenager. He was a man in a desperate situation. There was a sliver of breathable air near him on the floor, a little clearer, but still choked with ash. Sam heard screaming and a roar of fire as it moved up the building. Closer, closer. It was dark, congested. The room, he thought, was empty. He couldn't hear movement, couldn't see bodies. Just dark forms of table legs and overturned chairs and papers.

He tried to sit up, but dropped back to the floor, pushed down by the pain in his head and the stratum of smoke that filled the upper levels of the room. He decided to try to crawl out. He had no other options. Inch by inch, he moved forward on his belly, pulling with his forearms, pushing with his knees and toes, like a soldier under fire. He pulled a handkerchief from his pocket and tried to hold it to his mouth while he dragged himself along with the other arm. He pushed aside obstacles—a metal water pitcher, sheaves of paper, a leather chair—and then recoiled. His nose was almost touching what he knew must be a bald head. He poked it. No response.

"Hey," he rasped, "You okay?"

All he could see was the top of the head. His finger slipped around to the guy's neck, and he felt for the carotid. The surge in the artery was muted, barely noticeable, but there. He was alive, but likely not for much longer. Sam shimmied around the body and raised himself on an elbow to get a good look at this other survivor.

Frank Harrison. Dear God. Of everyone in that boardroom, of all those faithful colleagues he had sweat and bled with over the years, it had to be Frank.

For a moment, Sam remembered the humiliations, the gut punches, the black eyes, the money and homework assignments handed over, the achievements stolen, the shame and embarrassments.

And he wanted to leave him. He wanted to leave him in this room where Frank had been poised to take his company from him in one last *coup de grâce*. He deserved to burn. Nobody would blame him. No one would even know.

The image of his mother hovered in the cloud of smoke in front of him. "Love thy enemies, Samuel," she said sweetly.

He wanted to argue, to curse, to persuade her that she was wrong, that she didn't understand, that her biblical phrases slipped off the jagged edges of his memories without smoothing them. But then there was a single moment of absolute clarity as the indignities of a lifetime melted away in that fire. There was epiphany in the flames, the insight of mystics. He wanted to meet eternity unburdened, light and untouched by the weight of bitterness.

He took his handkerchief, tied Frank's hands together, and pulled them over his head. Frank's arms were wrapped around Sam's neck, so that the unconscious man hung under him as he crawled out of the boardroom, past the executive offices, through the cubicle farm, and around the receptionist's desk. It was harder and harder to breathe, to move. He stopped only when Frank was lifted out from under him by a firefighter. The first responder with the oxygen mask flipped Frank over his shoulder and moved into the stairwell. When his partner reached Sam, it was too late.

He would not have known, but the fifty-six minutes of burning were over. The South Tower collapsed, the crowning antenna riding the top of the disintegrating building down the massive swell of smoke and atomized architecture all the way to the foundation. The North Tower would follow a half-hour later. And with it, the body of Samuel A. Neville.

Clayton H. Ramsey

INTERVIEWS

Naming Difficult Things
An Interview with Annemarie Ní Churreáin

Annemarie Ní Churreáin shines as a literary descendant of such Irish poets as Nuala Ní Dhomhnaill, Paula Meehan, and Eavan Boland, to name a few. She strives to increase the space available to Ireland's women authors by examining the numerous ways certain Irish institutional systems, such as the Catholic Church, have tried to silence the voices of women over the last hundred years or so. One stark way these Irish institutions silenced women was through the mother and baby homes, which served as a form of incarceration of unmarried pregnant women, separating them from their children at birth and sending the children into the foster system. Through *Bloodroot* and her new collection, *The Poison Glen*, and in her service to Ireland's marginalized communities through the arts, Annemarie has broken that silence when necessary and given names to very difficult things.

This interview was conducted live over Zoom on February 20, 2021 and continued over email into May 2021.

Rumph: *Annemarie, first, I want to say I love the musicality of your name. In the United States, we don't often encounter last names like "Ní Churreáin." That probably sounds terrible with my accent.*

Ní Churreáin: That's a very noble attempt, as I've been called stranger things. The "Ní" in Churreáin, the "N-i-fada," means "daughter of." My brothers would be "O Churreáin," or "son of," instead of "Ní." I was raised as "Annemarie Curran," which is my English-language name. Many people in the Donegal Gaeltacht are raised with their English-language name. When I was growing up in the Gaeltacht in the 1980's, there was some residual hesitancy, or perhaps even shame, about using one's Irish name when it came to affairs of an official nature that involved interaction with those outside the community.

When I started to write and publish, I decided that I wanted to use my Irish-language name. Not only is it more interesting to me lyrically than is "Curran," but it speaks to my Gaeltacht identity. It's an act of reclamation. I realize it's a double-edged sword because a lot of people have trouble with the Irish pronunciation, even in Ireland, but I'm glad I made the decision. Names are special and complicated in my family because my father was adopted, so "Curran" or "Churreáin" is not his birth name. Also, a lot of my foster siblings would have had a sensitive decision to make about whether to use their birth names or change their names. As a child, I was keenly aware that a name carries special currency. As an adult, I'm aware of the patriarchy it perpetuates within Irish culture. In my poem "Doire Chonaire," I speak of how a name gets "passed down through the spear side / in underland streams that pulse with clear meaning / and thrive towards the lips."

Your poem, "Family Law," from your collection Bloodroot, *says, "Your name begins in Ruis and mine in Ailm." Does that line have a connection with your name, and what is the significance of it for you?*

One of the earliest forms of the Irish language was written in Ogham script, which is sometimes called "the tree alphabet." It was inscribed on bark and on stone. Each Ogham alphabet letter was associated with a tree. "Family Law" came about when my goddaughter was about six years old. She was making her First Holy Communion. During that time, she became anxious because other family members weren't following the traditional practices of the church, and we were not expressing our spirituality in the same way she was. I was tucking her into bed one night when she asked, "What do you believe in, and what is going to keep you safe from harm?" I went away and thought about it, and the poem is a response to her questioning. It conjures a belief system that is based around the physical landscape, rootedness, and pre-Christian traditions. Ogham is magical to me because it conveys the idea, historically speaking, that nature is in our language and that language is in our nature. Our language—the sound and the writing of it—is connected and bound up in the wild environment.

It is metapoetic in that way because it brings in these elements and makes them a part of the poem. Do you see it that way?

Definitely. Many of my poems interweave multiple realities. A lot of my work comes out of the physical landscape, and for me, the language and the built and wild environments are fundamentally intertwined. Sometimes, I work with Irish-language place names, which provide a gateway into history and myth, allowing a deeper understanding of that place through story. There is always the question of when to include a footnote about site information in a poem. My approach tends to be that I like to leave a little bit of mystery, leave a little bit for the reader to discover.

You mentioned that you stayed and studied in Ireland because it was important for you to reclaim the female voice as part of your writing and to retain and nourish your Irish heritage. As I understand, the first language you learned to speak was Irish, and English came a little later.

Yes, Irish is my first language. I grew up in the Gaeltacht. There's only a few Gaeltacht regions remaining in Ireland. These are geographical pockets, mainly along the coast, where the Irish language and customs are still alive. The language has been lingering in a precarious place for a long time. I don't know how much you know about it, but probably the biggest blow to the Irish language was the famine, which resulted in a lot of emigration. English rule in Ireland tried to stomp out the Irish language. All that said, it's still here. The revival is only a hundred years old. The pandemic has given us time to reflect on our lives and culture, and there is a resurgence of interest from people looking to learn how to speak it. We must not reduce Irish, or any language, to mere spoken words, as it is a whole way of life.

You'll often hear Irish people say, "I don't speak Irish. I wish I did, but I can't." Culturally we have a competency problem with it, and there may be some element of shame. The Gaeltachts were often poor areas. Certainly, when I was growing up, one would tend to switch over to English when speaking to someone in an official capacity. Irish was the language of the family and the community, which knew each other intimately and knew all the sorrows that went with the Gaeltacht community—the loss, the emigration, and the poverty. There was perhaps a sense of Irish being the heart language and English being the official language if you were required to represent yourself in the business world. To some degree, that still exists today. It's really important that I continue to do what I can on behalf of my mother tongue and that other people do as well because when a language is lost, so too is a whole perspective on life, of a way of being in the world.

I equally have that idea of it as a heart language, rightly or wrongly. Even in Ireland, there can be a sense among non-Irish speakers that speaking the Irish language is revolutionary or romantic. We have all these funny ideas about it, when really it is a lived, day-to-day, minority language. It's in this precarious place, but I feel hopeful for it. I've never felt more hopeful for it as I have during lockdown because we're seeing people in Ireland, and maybe worldwide, paying more attention to our surroundings, our landscape, our culture, and our heritage. Anytime I run a workshop that is Irish-language themed, people are just hungry for it. There's a real appetite for it in this country to reconnect with our rootedness through the language. I feel it's kind of flourishing at the moment.

It seems like the simple, personally democratic act of reclaiming and using your Irish name can be an important step to bring the traditions and the language back to life.

Absolutely. I live in Dublin at the moment, and it would be easy for me not to speak Irish. The majority of the people I know don't speak it. It's not a language I can use in my interactions with employers. It takes a real effort to be proactive and use Irish words in my emails, in my poems and workshops, or to extend that invitation to others to use Irish in their interactions with me. You have to put yourself behind it and say, "This is important because it's a beautifully unique and rich language that can never be replaced."

You mentioned English rule earlier. The penal laws that were in place, such as not permitting people to speak or write in the Irish language and requiring everything to be conducted in English, forced Ireland to adopt the English language and ways of life.

Recently, I spoke with the writer, Manchán Mangan, who launched a book titled *Thirty-Two Words for Field*. We spoke about all the knowledge and wisdom inherent in the Irish language that have to be learned again in English—caring for a landscape, knowing that your body is an extension of the landscape, looking after the environment, living healthily, and using sustainable ways. We have all of that in the Irish language built into our place names, in the folklore associated with plants and trees, and in the stories associated with sites. It provides for a way of seeing the world that cannot always be translated, which is at risk of becoming erased whenever a language burns out.

You're from Donegal. As I understand it, that is located in the northwest part of the country. For someone who's never visited Donegal, how would you describe it?

Well, Donegal, in Irish, is pronounced "doon-e-nal," which means "fort of the foreigners." It's a strange, wild, beautiful place that is challenging to live in because of the difficult weather there. There's no public train. It's quite isolated. It's had the highest levels of emigration. Despite all of that, it is the most rugged, beautiful, deeply haunted, and lived-in county. It's the land of giants, scholars, witches, and ghosts. One of the famous myths of the county is that of the battle between Balor of The Evil Eye and Lugh, the God of Light. I was raised on all of that magic. It's not like other parts of Ireland at all. When you go to Donegal, you're getting this really immersive experience, like going to an island. That's the best way I can describe it. If you go to the islands off Donegal, it's like going back in time. Out of the sorrow of these communities comes a deep sense of togetherness, of creativity, of an appreciation of beauty. You can't compare a living and thriving city, like Dublin, which keeps rebuilding and replenishing itself, to Donegal, where the oldest languages and customs are alive, the songs and the folklore. Every field has a story associated with it, every site. I often think the people I know there live in a perfect harmony with the seasons. It's wild living. It's a wild, strange place. The word "darklight" comes to mind when I think of Donegal. It has this compelling duality of unspoiled beaches alongside haunted islands. In summertime, because tourists are so few, it's just a playground with all the beautiful sites. If you find yourself out on the cliffs when that black rain comes in winter, it's frightening. Donegal gives the full blast of human experience.

You have spoken about a bog in Donegal that has rich traditions stemming from the masculine and religious perspectives, and that you want to reclaim the female story of that place. Why is that important for you, and why is that important for others to hear?

Much of the Donegal bogland upon which I grew up was inscribed with the patriarchal narratives of saints, scholars, mythological giants, monsters and male heroes and anti-heroes. Female figures were not central players or characters in these stories. But it was a place that gave me a keen sense of what lies buried just beneath any surface, of what may reappear at any time. The bog is a shifting landscape, constantly swallowing things up and spitting them back out. For anyone who has not grown up there, it may seem like a barren, bleak, difficult terrain. But I feel a deep connection with its bright-black magic. So, yes, of course, I want to explore my own experience as a woman through this place. It has been a lot of fun to write the female experience back into the community, back into the bog.

When you dig around in Irish pre-Christian mythologies and histories, of course, there are dynamic female figures there. They just didn't get any airplay. They just weren't made visible. Often, a fun thing for me to do in my writing is to engage with the landscape and do a feminist reading of it. Some of the poems I'm writing at the moment reference the myth of Balor of the Evil Eye, which is associated with the Poison Glen in Donegal. Balor, a King of the Fomorian Giants, locked his daughter Eithniu in a glass tower on Tory Ireland to prevent her from ever meeting a man. His plan failed, however, and Eithniu conceived a son named Lugh the God of Light, who eventually killed Balor. As you can see, the main players in this story were all male figures, so it has been interesting for me to spend some time considering the experience of Eithniu, looking at the subject of violence through the lens of her myth, and bringing her narrative into the light.

A few months ago, I read some fairy tales to some schoolchildren. I read them a traditional retelling of Balor of the Evil Eye, and we discussed the story. They had such illuminating thoughts. For example, they said that Balor should have had anger management counseling so that he could resolve his issues with his daughter, and the twelve maidens who locked Eithniu in the tower were bystanders to bullying and should have stood up for her. In our discussion together, we were able to bring contemporary dialogue about power structures to this really old myth. There's a long tradition of Irish language female writers reclaiming the female experience in Irish myth. Nuala Ní Dhomhnaill, for example, writes about Queen Medb (pronounced "Māv"). She has an incredible reimagining of Queen Medb's life and gives her a lot of power, sexuality, a strong personality, and dignity.

Queen Medb is not simply the woman who went to war, but she's a woman driven by a complex intellect and great sense of her abilities.

Everything you've said speaks to the influence that place has had on you as a writer, as a poet.

The Irish writer John Moriarty wrote, "Unless there's wildness around you, something terrible happens to the wildness inside you." Those words resonate with me. I don't mean "wild" as in "reckless." I mean that we're all these extensions of this unknowable, mysterious earth. We're all able to thrive and survive in ways that we've lost a connection with. We think we need technology, certain kinds of foods, or a certain amount of money. Capitalism has robbed us of the wisdom of our ancestors. What growing up in Donegal taught me is that we can flourish against the odds. Landscape, community, culture, and good health can sustain us. We had a large family, and my father was always looking for work. Like many of the fathers in my community, he had to go abroad to make ends meet, but I never thought the word "poor" described us well. Money aside, we were abundantly rich. It was a difficult grind for my parents but having gone through that and come out of that place, I feel it gave me life skills that have served me well. It gave me so much in terms of poetry, story, language, and music. Donegal taught me how to be in the world, how to be fearless, how to pick myself up, and how to make something out of little or nothing. I often think the rural working-class background in Donegal comes into play in my poems because I'm constructing and making something where there is nothing to begin with. I'm assembling. All my siblings are like that. We're the original self-starters. That's a Donegal thing, being gifted by the wild landscape.

That's the essence of poetry. From those who don't write or study poetry or have an appreciation for it as an art form, you often hear that it's inaccessible. They may not understand how you made the journey from beginning to end, taking disparate ingredients, figuring out how they fit together and how they relate to one another.

I'm the only poet in my family, but my sister is a singer, and my brothers all work in trade as carpenters, builders, and plumbers. We have a shared sensibility for the art of making. There are definite parallels to be drawn with the craft person who works with physical materials and the craft person who works with emotions and intellect and life experience.

In Ireland, there's such a deep appreciation of creativity. It's not unusual for everyone to have a favorite poet or to have a song to their name or to have someone in the family who makes some craft or art. I didn't realize how much a part of our culture that is. It must come out of that cultural oppression under the rule of the English because so much was taken away from you, you had to work with what you had left. You had to make beauty and transformative moments out of the scraps that were available to you.

That circles back to the reclamation of the autonomous individual. I'm reminded of Frank McCourt's Angela's Ashes, *set in Limerick. It also speaks to that idea that we're going to take these limited resources and do the best we can.*

I'm sure it's not culturally unique, but it's such a major aspect of Irish creativity and culture—the idea that you can't take a person's voice, you can't take their mind, and you can't take their soul. You can't even stamp out these traditions, despite the penal laws and history. Brigid's Eve is the last day of January. Her celebration is the first day of February. She was a pre-Christian goddess later claimed in the Catholic faith as a saint. Her wells can be found all over Ireland. So many people I know follow the customs of Brigid by putting out cloths in the yard on Brigid's Eve for the goddess to come invest the cloth with medicinal qualities. Ireland's managed to hold onto these

rituals, despite everything. What's not impressive about that?
Ireland has so many unique musical aspects about its culture, such as the Sean-nós, uilleann pipes, bodhran drums, and harp guitars.

The Sean-nós is very strong in Donegal. When any person in a small pub, typically an elderly man, starts up a Sean-nós song, the whole pub goes quiet. There's a mutual understanding that somebody needs to be heard, and it's really rude to talk over them. When you're a teenager having your fun at the pub and somebody starts singing, you're thinking, "Oh god, here we go." But I have so much respect for it now, an awareness that there are times that you just need to be still and silent and need to listen. The world has been losing sight of that in recent years. We're distracted and busy, and we have to be so productive all the time. Silence is a rich source of inspiration for me. I often use it in my own live readings. I believe moments of stillness, whether in a poem or in a packed venue, is a kind of protest, but also a gift to a reader or an audience. For women, it can be an act of reclamation. There's tremendous feeling in that moment when you can hear a pin drop, and you realize that we're all engaged in a deep act of listening. It's restorative, and for me, there's something healing in it. There's been so much silence around women's lives, a lot of dark history in what institutions of the Irish Church and State have done to women in Ireland, in imposing silence. There's something lovely to reclaim that silence and to make it a positive thing again. The Sean-nós silence around songs is a positive thing. I'm as interested in silence as I am in words and how they all work together, so it's interesting you brought up the Sean-nós.

As I've listened to your other interviews, it seems that Ireland is supportive of the arts. Is that accurate?

There's a deep appreciation in Ireland for the arts and creativity. There's no shame in saying you're a poet or an artist. It's not the same in other places. It's not seen as a failure of any kind. When I've gone abroad and said in different cultures that I'm a poet, people will say that their middle school child writes poems. In Ireland, the frame of reference for being a poet isn't just associated with early childhood or hobbies. Everyone knows who Heaney is. Most people have a favorite poem or song they know by heart. I would say we have good, robust levels of support. Is it on par with the support of the arts in someplace like Germany? It probably isn't. It's not a perfect infrastructure, but I'm proud that the country has the Arts Council. They're the agency that looks after government funding for the arts. Anyone can apply to the Arts Council and make their case. It's an open, transparent, and fair system.

Listen, I've been to other countries, and there isn't that funding, infrastructure, or support at all. Here, you can meet a publisher in person at any reading and introduce yourself. You can make an application to the Arts Council. You can access a certain level of funding for a Master of Philosophy degree. I did, for the M.Phil in creative writing. We're landing somewhere between the middle and the top of the ideal cultural support. For me, the important thing is that the endeavor is culturally understood here, and people appreciate it. It wouldn't be unusual for the ordinary person who hasn't gone through third-level education, and isn't involved with the arts, to appreciate what you do. They wouldn't feel threatened by it. Perhaps, French culture is like that as well. They have a comfort with saying whether they like a painting or don't like a painting. That's a generalization, but my experience of having been in Paris is that people are vocal about their opinions on art and literature. They don't feel like they have to be a writer or artist to share those opinions, and that's how it should be. Nobody owns poetry. Everyone has a stake in it. I'm glad to live in a country that does not think I have made bad career decisions and therefore deserve to be a starving artist.

You spent some time in Florida at the Jack Kerouac house in Orlando. How long were you there?

69

In 2014, I was the Fall Writer-in-Residence at the Kerouac House. I just loved it because it's really refreshing to go into a landscape when you know nothing about it and have no expectations. I didn't know anything about Florida. To some extent, the exposure we get in the media to Florida or that I see on my social media is swayed in one direction, so I was getting a certain political narrative. When I got there, the landscape was thrilling with Spanish moss hanging from the trees, neon lights on the downtown Orlando lakes at midnight, and the sound of the limpkin against the warm night skies. I spent a lot of time on the St. John's River looking at tribal sites, learning about different tribes, and spending time in the oldest pieces of culture I could find. I met talented people. I had an astonishing time connecting in an emotional way with the lushness and greenness of the landscape.

I've read that you love Flannery O'Connor. What is it about her that appeals to you, and are there any other Southern Gothic writers who have influenced you?

I started reading O'Connor during my M.Phil, and I hadn't heard of her before that. Her courage to expose the ugly sides of humanity struck me, as did her fearlessness in bearing witness and going to the difficult side of humanity. I was impressed with her moral wrangling with frightening questions and the idea that the story is the moral. I couldn't believe what I was reading. In a way, it felt different from anything I read in the context of Irish literature or tradition. Listening to her voice on those old recordings, her accent, I was gripped. She's quite an enigmatic, fierce woman who's unconcerned with being liked. She's a flawed person with flawed social perspectives. Her stories remain complex and challenging, which makes them difficult to forget.

I went through my whole education in primary and secondary school without really hearing much from women writers at all. I had to go pursue a master's degree to connect with Irish female writers. To see what she was doing in Milledgeville, Georgia, at that time makes me think of her and Raymond Carver on their thrones, the queen and king, both such difficult and flawed people, dogmatically writing themselves into history with their stories.

I love Raymond Carver, as well. Unless you took literature in Ireland, Raymond Carver wasn't well known. I didn't grow up in a bookish house at all. It was rural, working class. Stories came in through the radio and our one black and white television station. Stories were passed around in the community through the oral tradition. They came in through the tabloids, which fed us stereotypical and patriarchal gender archetypes. I'm still interested in how women are represented in the redtops or tabloids. It gave me rich material to draw from when I began writing. I didn't have proper access to writing by women until I went to do my M.Phil. So, Flannery O'Connor has a special place in my heart because she was one of those first influences. Sylvia Plath, as well. I'm sure that's the case for a lot of people. Emily Dickinson was maybe the only other female poet on my secondary school English curriculum in the 1990s.

I understand you teach in the prison system. Are you still doing that, and how did you come to be involved in that process?

I'm an active panelist on the Irish Writers in Prisons Scheme funded by the Arts Council of Ireland. My job is to provide guest workshops on an ad-hoc basis to students within the prison education service. When you asked this question, I was thinking about this quote from James Joyce, who said that all poetry is an act of revolt against actuality. The work that I do in prison is an extension of the endeavor, within my wider practice, of bearing witness and of sharing creative space with people living in the care of the Irish State. I'm interested in the subject of the incarcerated voice. What happens to someone's voice who is in the care of the state. How is it diminished? How is it shaped by silence? Who does it speak to? I enjoy spending time with students in prisons. It's probably the work I find most challenging and most nurturing. It's soul-expanding work unlike any other. When you go into the prison, you're getting the full blast of the human experience—grief, sorrow, shame, regret, loneliness. To see how people survive at their darkest moment is impressive to me. Our prison system in some ways is probably not as cruel as prison systems in other places, but the physicality of the prisons is pretty cruel. Prisons are cold in winter. They have rats. Up until a few years ago, there was a slopping out system. It is a challenging environment to be in—to see people under those conditions get themselves up and ready, bring their page they've been working on, and come to a workshop, when maybe they've lost connections to their family and children. Sometimes, you meet people and they've lost everything. In the worst-case scenarios, they're never going back to the life they had before. Even they will come to the workshop and have enough hope left in them that something they could say might be important or might have a transformative quality. It leaves me feeling like I've seen the best of humanity.

People have asked me if I'm frightened going into prisons. It's hard to explain. People bring the best of themselves to a workshop because they're bringing their creativity. They're not bringing their crime or the parts of themselves that committed the crime. They're bringing the hopeful part of themselves, and sometimes they're bringing a really vulnerable part, as well. I just see the best of my students by virtue of the environment we're in. What a gift it is to facilitate for people the naming of experiences they've never named before, to say things aloud. I've had writers tell a story about their lives that they've never told anyone before. That is so inspiring to be around. I miss it in these times because it's a reminder of the transformative qualities of writing. It's such a primitive thing to make a mark with your body or make a sound. In most cases, people can't take that away from you. It's a lovely reminder going into prisons that language is important, writing is transformative, and people generally are impressive in their ability to survive.

INTERVIEWS

A lot of the poems in *Bloodroot* were about breaking silence and naming things that are difficult, and they're really focused on people who have been victimized by violence or crime. It's been so rich for me to sit across the table from somebody who has perpetrated a violent crime and think about it with them in the picture as well. That's definitely part of the new collection, *The Poison Glen.* My thinking has expanded and in the picture is some kind of deeper awareness or engagement with the idea of perpetration or the perpetrator. That's been an important step for me. That came out of the prison experience for sure. It's a two-way thing. In the prisons, I always hope the students will learn and grow and the poetry is going to give them hope, but they're always teaching me how to write about these subjects. It's a good match. I'm sure it's not for every writer. There are many writers who would not want to go to prisons, but there's a tradition in Ireland of writers going into prisons and writing about prisons. Who was it that wrote the Mountjoy Prison song, "The Auld Triangle," Brendan Behan? It's been a good experience for me.

Do you see that the Irish female voice has been an imprisoned voice throughout time? Do you see a connection between people who have been incarcerated not having a voice in society and women in general not having a voice in society?

I think the Roman Catholic Church's influence working in tandem with the state over the last hundred years has a lot to answer for. Former Irish prime minister and president De Valera, in cahoots with Archbishop McQuaid, were the architects of this new country in which it was written into the Constitution that a woman's place would be in the home. This created the sense of women and their work as secondary and unequal to that of men. A hundred years is only a blip in time. We're a new state, a young state, and we've yet to harvest and carry forward the best of ourselves under pre-Christian laws and try to integrate that wisdom and knowledge into our ways of living today. Yes, I would say that women's voices have been incarcerated over the past hundred years in Ireland. Some evidence exists to suggest that under old Irish Brehon Law, women—while still unequal at that time in Ireland—enjoyed at least some benefits that do not exist today. Prior to Catholicism in Ireland, there was a history of worshipping the feminine divine. I don't know if you've heard of the Sheela Na Gigs, but these are old stone carvings found around Ireland. They're mysterious, erotic, figurative carvings of naked women displaying an exaggerated vulva. There was something else in this country before all the conditions were put into place to silence and erase women. I think we'll reconnect with all of that in the coming of years. I feel hopeful we will.

Does this relate to Ireland as a whole with its struggle for independence, its struggle to have its voice in the world free of British rule or free of the influence of the Catholic Church?

Irish artists do a stunning job of representing Ireland on a world stage. Irish art keeps on surviving and thriving, even during the worst times, even during the pandemic. I'm just mesmerized by the new interest that my poetry students have in Irish language voices and translation and how, as writers and artists, we've used this pause in ordinary routines to look at old traditions, customs, and rituals. Over the past eighteen months, I've started visiting ancient pagan wells and writing about them. It's in our blood to go on regardless, to find a way to innovate. That spirit, which will not be brutalized, manages to reinvent itself over and over again.

How do you see the trajectory of Irish poetry now and into the near future, to the extent you have a crystal ball in the room with you?

I see the Irish literary canon being replenished by the inclusion of new poets who were born in another culture and moved here, who are of a non-Irish or mixed ethnicity. The so-called "New Irish" will provide a richness that's exciting. To see these new poets, some with an ear for other languages and cultures, it wakes everyone up and keeps us vital.

Ireland has, historically, had a great love of the lyric poem. We're seeing a new space being carved out by writers who are doing something different with the lyric poem, doing something more innovative. I'm thinking about Kimberly Campanello, who's Irish-American. She has a book called *MOTHERBABYHOME*, in which she used archival material, including reports and official records, to make poems on the subject of the Tuam Mother and Baby Home in Galway. That's not something we've seen in Ireland before. It's not just culturally that we're being replenished, but linguistically, emotionally, and psychically. The last twenty years in Ireland have witnessed a rejuvenation of the spoken word poetry. All of that live performance is mostly dormant now, given the pandemic, but it is being carried over into online spaces. I think that will continue. The poet Nuala Ní Dhomhnaill says of the spoken word culture in Ireland that it's like "a plumbline into the subconscious." I identify with that and with the idea of the poem told, carried on breath, and conveyed straight out of the body, into the air, in a public space, as a way of understanding who and what we are.

The Irish lyric poem made for the page by the white male has been the bread and butter of the Irish cultural scene, but now, there's more visibility for the voices of women, for people of color, and for the "New Irish." We're always bemoaning technology and the internet and how it's diminished our quality of reading, but the reality is that it's also been quite good for poetry. There have been a lot of gifts with it—access to new audiences, access to experimentation, space for previously marginalized writers. There's a small Irish trans library archive now.

Thinking about the new voices breaking into the Irish literary canon, there's probably going to be a lot of beauty and resilience that emerges from the Direct Provision system, as dark as it is.

It's all too easy in Ireland to fall into the trap of thinking of Black Lives Matter only in the context of what is happening in the U.S. They're not thinking about it in the context of Ireland's Direct Provision system, in which many people of color are incarcerated. Racism exists in Ireland. It's important we don't romanticize that suffering, which is lived daily. There will be a range of voices that come out of that system. Beauty can coexist alongside anger, hurt, and outrage, and we're just beginning to hear some of the voices who have or are surviving the Direct Provision system in Irish poetry. The institutional violence against women in Ireland is terrifying, like the Magdalene Laundries, those penal institutions where "unfit" women and girls were enslaved and required to perform labor to financially benefit religious orders of the Catholic Church. This practice ended not that long ago, within our lifetime.

The author of *Republic of Shame*, Caelainn Hogan, performed extensive research on the history of the mother and baby homes and found a home, located in Donegal, actually, that did not close until 2006. Sadly, the 2021 Mother and Baby Homes Report only investigated a small number of the homes. The shocking figures you're seeing related to that report are only the tip of the iceberg. We're still processing it and understanding this part of ourselves. It's undoubtedly a dark part of the Irish psyche. It's postcolonial. The structures that were there for the poorhouses and workhouses during the time of the famine, brought by the English, were adapted by the Irish Church and State to house vulnerable women, unwed mothers, and their children. That kind of incarceration or holding pen for the vulnerable people of Ireland has been there for a long time.

One of the most recent iterations of the holding pen model is the Direct Provision system. People coming into Ireland looking for asylum are signed into temporary accommodation, without the right to work, and placed under curfew and granted only a very limited allowance on which to live. The hotels associated with this system are grim and overcrowded. In the system, people are forced to put their whole lives on hold, sometimes for years. Children are born into that system, and they've never known what it's like to have social freedom. It's a perpetration of a social violence.

Speaking of Irish institutional systems, you had a lot of foster siblings. That was one way English came into your life as a child, such as through inspector reports and interacting with officials. How did this inform your writing?

First of all, fosterage is an old part of Irish pre-Christian culture. There has been a long tradition of children moving between families to build alliances and to provide children with access to training and mentoring. Now, the foster care system looks different. It's overcrowded and underfunded. We have a shocking number of children in foster care for such a small country. There is evidence to suggest that we're not resourcing families to stay together, that we're not skilled enough at removing problems, instead of children, from families. Fostering taught me a lot about power dynamics, about the silence that can exist around trauma, about bearing witness, about using language in a transformative way. All of that came into my poetry. My family started fostering when I was around eleven years old. Up until that point, Irish was the everyday spoken language. As a foster sister, I lived with people who were carrying trauma, carrying secrets, who experienced things and didn't have the language to express their realities. Sometimes, kids only want to confide in each other. I grew up very quickly. English became more present in the household almost overnight.

Today, in my poetry, the separated mother and child is a recurring theme, along with the state and how it interferes or how the state lands in a family and how vulnerable people experience that. How does the state intersect with wildness? How does the influence of the state intersect with spirituality? It was such a landmark event in my life that, suddenly, we were caregivers of the state. That remains in my poetry today.

It's brought up interesting questions for me as well. One of the things I'm thinking about at the moment is the ethics of writing. How do you bear witness to the experiences and sorrows of other people? Where is the line in exploiting that? How do you mindfully engage with history and honor it, name it, tell it, and bring it out into the light so the world can be transformed? How do you also ensure that you're not perpetrating another violence? Ireland has experienced significant social changes, recently. In 2015, there was the Marriage Equality Referendum, followed by the Repeal the Eighth Campaign in 2018, and the release of the Mother and Baby Homes Report in 2021. Everyone is thinking about the Irish psyche and trauma and how important it is to name things, but how do you do that in a way that's responsible and constructive? Those questions were with me from a young age. I have a poem called "Sisters," which is dedicated to my foster sisters. I really wanted to write a poem for them and about my experience of living with over thirty foster sisters. I had to question how to write a poem and ensure that these girls, these sisters, are represented in a way that's not exploitive. I eventually came upon a device that worked for me.

In the poem, I change the name of every girl to the name of a powerful female figure from Ireland's historical or mythological past. That means I gave each girl the name of a powerful woman so that the poem didn't perpetrate another violence by exposing and laying bare the traumas of another person. To some extent it's exposing and it's laying something bare, but it's also investing them with power by saying, "I'm going to give you the name of someone who survived and who endured, and her name can be a vehicle through which hope is possible." In the same poem, I ask myself the question, "Will I be loved?" It felt necessary for me to inhabit my own vulnerability, and to expose myself, if I was going to bear witness to the difficulties of their individual lives.

How do you bring these things to light without causing more violence or perpetuating that cycle? It's a hard thing to do.

There's no easy answer. One of the things I'm always thinking about is that I need to bring myself to the poem. At the end of "Sisters," I turn the text in on myself to reveal a question I have about myself. It's really important for writers, if you're going to explore someone else's story, to make sure you're exploring your own as well. In an Irish poetry workshop, I had a young student who wanted to write about gun violence in the context of the Black Lives Matter movement in the U.S. I was reminded that the challenge for any writer is to ask yourself why and how you're drawn to a subject and to make a connection that is real for you. In Ireland, we have a massive problem with gun violence, but it's not easy to look at the subject up close, in the context of the social and cultural landscape you're living in. But that examination and place of connection may be where the poem is waiting to be found. That's the challenge—to understand what you're writing about or want to write about in the context of your own lived experience. At the beginning of my writing journey, I was making poems about the physical landscape, about herblore and the folklore attached to plants and trees. The more closely I began to look at these wild spaces, the more I began to observe the interruption caused by the state and by man-made institutions in the landscape. I felt drawn to monuments, graves, and derelict buildings. I found myself strangely compelled by the subject of the mother and baby homes. But why? It took me a while to realize that my grandmother's story was haunting me.

In 1951, she gave birth to my father in a home and was forced to give him up for adoption. The weight of that story, and the impact of those events on my life, was only fully revealed to me through the process of writing poems. In the act of writing, you cannot escape yourself. You have to face your demons. Similarly, I had to ask myself why I wanted to write about Ann Lovett, the fifteen-year-old schoolgirl who died giving birth in 1984. Why do I want to write about these women who lost their children? I had to dig into my own family history and realize there's an intergenerational trauma there. That's a painful place to go within yourself, but there's no other way of doing it. You can't hang yourself on someone else's story and hope that washes. At some point, you need to look inward to your own story and do that exploratory work. It's tricky and takes time and perseverance.

Is the poem "Intervention" in Bloodroot *tied to that experience for you?*

In the poem "Sisters," I made sure that I anonymized the stories as much as I could by interweaving them and giving the sisters different names, but the poem "Intervention" references the violence perpetrated upon one particular sibling. By and large, the foster siblings I had were often in care because of neglect, which can be tied to poverty, addiction, or illness. Sometimes, there were children who were in foster care because they came from violent or abusive homes. Certainly, where there's abuse like that, it stays with you. As an eleven-year-old in the eighties, I was sheltered from a lot of what was happening in the world. It was pre-internet. We were really a bit naïve as to the violence people perpetrated on each other. It was quite a shock with those stories coming into the home for me at a young age. I definitely logged them, picked up information on the grapevine, put an ear to a door, flipped through a report that was lying around. Children speak to each other when they won't speak to counselors or social workers. My siblings shared stories with me that never got aired in court.

When I wrote *Bloodroot*, it was important for me to honor some of that and to name it. I started writing the collection, and initially, there were no poems in it about my relationships with my foster siblings. That became problematic for me. These are kids who were often marginalized and made invisible and shuffled around a system. I thought that by excluding them from the book, I was repeating that marginalization, that erasure.

Was writing Bloodroot *healing in any way for you?*

I remain a bit wary of the word "healing" when it comes to books or literature because writing is not curative. It was definitely transformative. When I started writing *Bloodroot*, I thought I was going to write a book about the physical landscape and folklore attached to trees and plants and the wild beauty I grew up with in Donegal. I was braced for poems about wild weathers and coastal living until the writing began to steer me down an unexpected path. The more attention I paid to the landscape, the more I began to observe shrines, ruins, graves, and the traces of buildings which had once shaped the lives of vulnerable Irish women and children. This is the magic of landscape. It throws back at you the strange reflection of your own lived experience. Writing *Bloodroot* was often a dark and troubling experience. I did not always know if I should continue the journey. I still cannot say if it was, in the end, healing, but something in me did become transformed. The book is a record, I think, of a changing voice, of a changing state.

I wonder if there is any other way of making art. You have to risk the unknown and make yourself vulnerable to the process. I can understand why some people don't want to do that, but that's the job of the artist: to name the difficult things, things other people don't want to say, to bring the dark parts of humanity into the light and transform them into something beautiful and truthful. I suppose having written *Bloodroot*, I know much more about who I am. Would I want to write it all over again? Definitely not.

Jerry Rumph

Side Hustle and the Energy of Your Heart
An Interview with Michael Lucker and Carey Scott Wilkerson

Reinhardt University: Who or what were your early influences that resonated with you to become a writer?

Wilkerson: Well, I can tell you that early on, I wanted to write plays, but I hadn't read very many. In fact, I'd only read a dramatization of *Hard Times*. I like murder mysteries a lot so my early attempts for the stage were these very hackneyed, clichéd, bumbling, irresponsibly plotted, drawing-room, five-character murder mysteries. However, I did find that I had a knack for comic lines, which begins to shape something inside a text. And if you discover that you can be funny or that you can be dark or engage something surreal, if there's a tonality, a harmonic that you can hit, that becomes the way you shape a text. So, I started writing plays even before I'd read many plays. Later, of course, the decision of it became the harmonic overtone series, a pretentious claim that happens to be true. When I read *Oedipus* in high school, I thought that I'd seen something really vast and hurtful and absurd. And of course, the image of *Oedipus* gouging out his own eyes really stuck with me. I confess it was probably that, along with Kurt Vonnegut's *Slaughterhouse-Five*, that made me want to write.

Lucker: *The Six Million Dollar Man. Starsky & Hutch. The Rockford Files.* That was my literature, growing up. I wasn't much of a reader. I just became enamored with the television. I have this echo still in my head—my dad always saying, "Sit back from the television, you're going to go blind!"—because I was always right up on the box, trying to feel like I was in the middle of it. When I was twelve or thirteen, I went to Perimeter Mall down in Dunwoody and I saw *Raiders of the Lost Ark*. I literally remember stumbling out of the theater with my mom, and I said, "That's what I want to do with my life." It was just a strange, circular, serendipitous moment when my first real big gig in L.A. was working on *Indiana Jones and the Last Crusade*. It took me a few years to get from *Raiders* to *Last Crusade*, but fortunately, it took a while for Steven [Spielberg] to get there, too.

When I started doing all this teaching, people said, "You should write a book on screenwriting." I wrote *"Crash! Boom! Bang!: How to Write Action Movies."* It was released in Barnes & Noble across the country and the first place I ever saw it was at the Barnes & Noble at Perimeter Mall. I bought it! Then I walked out and looked to the right. And about a hundred yards away was the movie theater where I saw *Raiders of the Lost Ark*.

CSW: *Crash! Boom! Bang!* does for that genre what *Save the Cat!* did for action romantic comedies.

What was the most difficult and the easiest part of transitioning from screenwriting to novel writing?

ML: Tense was the biggest one. When I made the decision to write a novel, I emailed one of my former Emory creative writing students, who's now an editor of a big publishing house in New York, and she said to write in past tense. I was like, "All right, I'm just gonna bite the bullet and cross over to the dark side." So I started writing in past tense. In screenplays, each page is a minute, so at 120 pages it's a two-hour movie, right? You don't have time and space to spend two pages describing this wonderful room. You got two lines or three lines—groovy drapery, some paintings that look like they cost more than my house, the carpet and the fireplace. You kind of set it up, but in a novel, I have to sit and describe stuff. That was hard for me. The dialogue came easy to me as a screenwriter because I know how to write dialogue. The first chapter is more descriptive, but as the book evolves, I start falling into my Bruce Willis-Mel Gibson witty banter vernacular and it pretty quickly becomes quippy. The other thing that helped me was my understanding of how story works, and plot, and structure.

With a screenplay, you only have like two lines for description. Where is that line between you, as the screenwriter, and the director?

ML: Directors don't like being told how to direct, so when people take screenwriting workshops and classes, they all want to know, "Where does the camera terminology go? Where does the lingo go? Where do I put zoom in, pan, tilt, fade?" You don't put that in screenplays. You describe it, just like you would describe it when you're writing a novel, just more concisely. The director will come in and figure out where he wants to put the camera, how he wants to tell the story, through whose eyes we want to see the story. For the most part, you will find that novelists adapt really well to screenwriting. I've worked with a lot of novelists who want to adapt their own novel into a screenplay. You just have to learn how to consolidate, consolidate, consolidate. That's it! Your sense of imagery and theme and point of view, all the things you're learning, will serve you well.

Realistically, is there an age limitation with that? A lot of times the younger you get started, the better shot you have at things in industry work.

ML: Does age or locale affect your ability to break into the film and television industry? Yeah. But it's not insurmountable. Frankly, COVID's helped, Zoom's helped. All the executives that work at Warner Bros., Fox, TriStar, Columbia, who used to be in those halls every day, they're now back in Connecticut and in New Jersey, working out of their office in their house. The world's changed a lot in the last year or two or three, really. You don't all have to be in the room. A good buddy of mine is a writer on *The Blacklist.* And for the last two years, the writers are all over the country. They just need to be ready at ten a.m. Eastern Time in the writers' room where they may spend six hours on Zoom.

If we write a good novel, then get it published, and we want to try to get it adapted to a movie, how do we get movie companies interested in it?

ML: The first thing you should know is 50% of movies come from novels. If you think about needing to write an original screenplay— no, just write your book, and you've got just as good a chance of selling your book to a studio. Chances are, though, they'll love you as the novelist and they'll want to hire somebody like me who's written fifty screenplays to come in and adapt it. I mean, you get paid. I get paid. So, it's a win-win. Frankly, people are asking me, "Are you gonna write the screenplay for your novel?" "Hell, no." I'm gonna sit back and watch them argue over what to do about it. I'll help them if they want, but I love the idea of being a novelist. Right now, there are seventy-two film and television series shooting in the state of Georgia. It's usually somewhere between sixty and seventy. There's a lot of people here now that work in film and television. If you end up building relationships with somebody around here at a function or a workshop or a bar or whatever, you can say, "Hey, I wrote a book. I think it'd be a good movie." Everybody knows everybody in Los Angeles. If they're an actor, they have an agent, and their agent works down the hall from the literary agents. It all works on relationships. I know you guys learn about that here and talking about building those connections. It's not easy. But neither is anything worthwhile. Be focused on what you want and pursue it with your passion.

I want to ask you about Slaughterhouse-Five. *What was it about that novel—?*

CSW: The Vonnegut voice, of course. It's that spare, enormously sophisticated literary voice, the development of some black humor, dark, absurd humor, coming out of the 50s into the 60s. Think of Joseph Heller, Robert Coover, Thomas Pynchon, all of those figures who were developing a kind of ironic sensibility that tilted toward the absurd, which allowed the worlds of given reality and fantasy to mix freely. That's what really grabbed my attention with Kurt Vonnegut. Also, there are UFOs in it. For me, that really works. And, incidentally, I don't wish this to run contrary to any of the great editorial advice that you've received, which is absolutely correct, but I think that the present tense still has a future.

ML: I don't even know, what percentage of novels are written in present tense?

CSW: *Slaughterhouse-Five* is in the present tense. *Gravity's Rainbow* is in the present tense. I think that the present tense does have a kind of elegance and immediacy to it that's beautiful. A lot of students want to write first person because it's a comfort zone, and I like third person because it's a challenge, it makes you the narrator, a little bit distant in some regard. Therefore, you're able to describe more, and you're not just describing what you're seeing through this lens, and the reader can see everything around that narrator. I think first person is being published because, in a way, it's safer. Safer than third person.

ML: So, there's limitations and challenges to writing in first person.

It depends too on how much you need to reveal about your protagonists and how much you need to go into the protagonist's mind. If you need to treat them on the same level as all of your other characters and you need to reveal more about other characters, you couldn't do that with first person. This is where the writer's strength with dialogue would come in. Third person makes exposition easier, because in first person, you can only see what the character sees, you can only be where they are. In third person, you can go anywhere, be omnipotent.

ML: That's kind of how it is in writing screenplays. You gotta show it. You can't be talking about what happened. If Bruce Willis walks into the room with a gun, this is the time to talk about what Bruce Willis does with the gun in the room. In a movie, you have to show it, because we're watching it on screen. Going off on tangents, going inside the character's mind. How are we supposed to know what Bruce Willis is thinking about when he's on screen? In a novel, you can do all that.

Michael, as far as the industry itself, what are your thoughts on how things have transitioned, with Netflix and Amazon starting their own production companies and buying screenplays and producing originals?

ML: The quantity of content that is being sought has exploded exponentially. It's good news for all you guys, because everybody needs content. No one's getting paid as much as they used to, but there are more jobs. In the old world, there were screenwriters writing movies, and then there were television writers writing television. Now, everybody's doing a little bit everything. Everybody's got a hustle and a side hustle, and everybody's writing stuff. If you're a writer, write. Be a writer. Write novels, write poems. Just keep writing. What's nice about film and television is that it pays well and there are lots of opportunities. If that's something that interests any of you, I think it's remiss for you not to at least explore it. It seems weird when you're sitting in Waleska, Georgia, thinking, "How do I become a screenwriter when Hollywood's out there?" But I have to tell you, I came from Chamblee, Georgia. Everybody comes from somewhere. The opportunities are out there.

Scott, you're a professor at Columbus State. As a professor and a writer, do you cross the lines where you bring your own work into your classroom? Or do you keep those separate?

CSW: If my students ask me about my own work, I will certainly tell them, but different people in the creative writing track have different philosophies about this. I always feel very self-conscious about presuming to recite my CV to my students, but if they ask me about a project, I'll certainly answer the question.

Do you put your work on your syllabus?

CSW: I would never do it. Some do. It feels gross to me. I have colleagues who do it. I do worry about the ethical implications of such a thing. Now, there's no problem if a colleague happens to say, you know, "I have this new book, maybe look at it," and then I could program it into my syllabus, but even that feels like an ethical issue about getting your students to buy your book.

LM: I'll share an alternative view since many of you might be going into academia, if you're not in it already. If you want to publish a book, the publisher is going to say, "Oh, you're a nice person. You're a good writer. What are you going to do to get this book out in the world? How many followers you got on Instagram? How many followers you got on TikTok? How many followers you got on Facebook?" If you don't think that's real, you are naïve. "How are you going to get it out there?" When you say, "I'm a professor of screenwriting at this institution," they're like, "All right, good! Will you use it in your classes? Do we know we're gonna sell three hundred copies a year between your workshops and your classes? Do you speak? Are you on panels? Are there places that you can talk about your book to help the sales?" Because it ain't just about you, and it ain't just about your book—it's about the marketability that you bring as the author. A lot of authors don't want to hear about that. We just want to sit in our little room and drink our coffee and type. The world is changing. You bringing some of that audience to the table is a great strength for you getting your book published.

CSW: Let's take a moment to view the question of literary versus non-literary. On one hand, we probably all couldn't say precisely what is literary and what is non-literary, although we could describe some of the characteristics, the received view of what those two things are. I think the distinctions in the end are illusory. What really matters is that you do what is right for you, what is congruent to the energy of your heart. Let others decide whether it's literary. Let others decide what shelf they're going to put it on. Do you know what I mean? Just do what you need to do. Harry Crews is an example of a writer who's not literary. The forward-facing aspect of Crews' books is not literary in the received sense, but he's certainly appreciated by a literary world. Hunter S. Thompson has some of that as well, although I think Thompson was probably more self-consciously aware of the dual audience that he had. I would just say, write what you need to write. For me, I have no choice except to do what I can do. Sometimes I don't really know what it is until it's done. You may have a different view of this. I just sometimes don't quite know what it is I'm working on until I'm in it, working on it, or until it's done.

Scott, if you could only write poetry or plays until you die, which one would you pick?

CSW: I'm gonna give you a difficult answer. I would fuse the two. I've been working a lot in opera for the past two or three years. And it seems to me that those—

A loophole. (laughter)

CSW: Yeah, that's right, a loophole. If I could somehow find a way to finance experimental operas for the next twenty-five years and just write librettos for those projects, I would do it. Now, we're indulging in fantasy here. In five years, I might decide that's no good anymore. But that's how I feel about it right now.

Do you know of the Hudson Guild? The Elephant Theatre did *Seven Dreams of Falling*, and one of the producers told me that they had a pile of scripts and that they wouldn't have produced my play if they hadn't liked it, but the only reason they really picked it up to begin with was that they liked the title. Yeah, it's a retelling of the Icarus myth, of course. It's seven visions of Icarus falling with different kinds of results. We had a really nice production, and it was successful, whatever that means, right, in the Hudson Guild, in a small theater, black box, set on Santa Monica Boulevard, during the Fringe Festival. Whatever that finally means. But it attracted enough attention so that there was another production in Oregon. Then there was a reading online somewhere. And a composer in Georgia was looking around for a librettist for his opera, so they were looking around for a librettist, and the reviewer at the *Huffington Post*, whose review caused my play to sell out its run, said that I should look at the character of Ariadne and do something with that story. I did a small opera workshop with that, and the composer in Georgia saw that workshop and contacted me. Since then, I've done four. I'm not writing the music, only the libretto.

Collaboration—how do these people find each other? Is it a network of things?

CSW: Yeah, that's right. You got to put it on your social media, let people find you. I have to say that Michael's observations about social media are right on the money.

ML: I love the writing. I do not love the movie business. That's why I decided to write a novel. Twenty years after I graduated from Boston University, I connected with the woman who was the academic counselor in the communications program. I reached out to her because I started to teach and she said, "Michael, I remember when you were here. You said you wanted to write novels and teach college." I've kind of come full circle. When I landed back in Georgia, it felt like home. I felt whole and happy. There were nice people and there were seasons. Green on the trees. The Reinhardt campus is like an oasis to me. I was surprised at how fulfilling it would be to teach. Every time I teach or speak, whatever, it's really rewarding. Hollywood's not like that.

Do you remember your conversation with that woman twenty years ago?

ML: I vaguely remember. I remember loving college, the intellectual stimulation and the healthy discourse of ideas. I loved learning, and

I loved teaching. Then I went out to L.A. and just had my soul raked through the dirt. Every day, you'd go in and argue with somebody about whether it should be a black guy or a white guy, night or day, city or country. It happens when you get to the producers. It happens when you get to the directors. It happens when you get to the studios. A friend of mine, who's a really successful sitcom writer in Los Angeles, said that he gets paid really well. Half of his money is to write, while the other half of his money is to deal with all that other stuff. If you go in with that perspective, knowing that it may not all be fun, then you might be able to stomach it a little more readily than others.

Is it possible to get published by smaller publishers—so you don't have to go to New York, where people are mean? (laughter)

ML: Frankly, there's plenty of people in the room that can answer better about going the way of novel writing and publishing than me, and I look forward to learning from them. But your publisher really needs to be in New York or based through New York. There are publishers everywhere, but they may not have the same marketability, the same reach.

CSW: In some ways, although my experience is entirely different from Michael's, I can agree with this. The industry itself, I'm thinking of the theatre industry, and particularly staging operas, the fundraising side of it—just the money—is grotesque and unpleasant and makes me unhappy. And as a librettist, I imagined naively that I would be left out of such conversations and I wouldn't have to participate in any of that nonsense, and it is a lot of nonsense, but projects must be financed, projects must be underwritten somehow. It means that I have to talk to donors because that's how these projects get done. Usually, there's a large donor base that finances everything so you can hire the orchestras, the conductors, and the singers. Even then they lose money. As well, there's a lot of government underwriting for all of this. That's something about which I've had to learn quite a lot, and in which I'm interested not at all. (laughter) You know what I mean?

I'd love to be able to do this without that. But, I'm not Stephen Sondheim. The name Carey Scott Wilkerson, *librettist*—people aren't out standing by street corners, saying, "You know what we really need is another experimental opera by that guy, and *then* we might finally be happy." (laughter) It isn't the case, so every project is a new slog. I do it because I love it. I don't know that I'm good at much else. So, I'm stuck with that. I mean, I can change the oil in a car, but I couldn't replace the computer. There's a way in which I'm caught up in the terms of the very problem that I have myself created, but when the house lights go down and the curtain goes up, and something's happening—you wrote it—when the spotlight hits and someone sings a note, there is a *frisson* that causes everything to evaporate.

ML: Not for me. I don't want to be in the theater when people are watching the movies. It kind of freaked me out to hear your reactions to my two chapters that I read tonight. It was so damn quiet! (laughter) What happens with scripts? I write it, then it goes off to all these other people, and they bring their time and energy and talent and experience to make it. It may not turn out to be what I expected. And I would say, everything that I've written that's been made into a film or TV series, I will watch it once. And I don't think I've gone back and watched anything again. I learned that from Steven [Spielberg], that he never goes to the theater to watch his movies. I'll never forget when I was with him when *Indiana Jones and the Last Crusade* just came out. I had been at the premiere for *Last Crusade* the night before with all the cast and crew, but Steven wasn't there. Well, there's this one moment when Indiana Jones is trying to find the tunnel beneath a quiet library, and he's banging a post, but he does it right when the old guy in the library is stamping the books. Steven just had one question, "Did they laugh, when the old guy was stamping?" (laughter) I said, "Yeah, it was hilarious!" And he said,

"Cool." That was it! Then, we went in to work on the next movie. He doesn't like being in the theater. In fact, he doesn't read the reviews. He taught me not to read them as well. We don't need all that in our heads.

Is there a script that you've written where you thought one thing, and the one time you saw it, it turned out to be the complete opposite of what you imagined it was gonna be?

ML: Often. It's one of the reasons I left Los Angeles. (laughter) One of the hardest things about writing movies and television is that you pour your heart and soul and pain into those pages in order for them to really come to life and be rich with power. And then you've got to let your baby go. It's really hard because writers are an emotional sensitive sort. It's kind of what makes us good writers.

What was the hardest script you had to experience that with?

ML: *Vampire in Brooklyn* was really hard, which was my first movie. I was twenty-seven when it came out, and I was really excited because I loved Eddie Murphy—*48 Hrs.*, *Beverly Hills Cop*, and *Trading Places* were some of my favorite movies. The movie turned out not to be at all what we wanted. We were so excited because we were living on macaroni and cheese, and we got the job and wrote our hearts out and we got the script made, but the studio was Paramount, who did *Beverly Hills Cop*. They wanted the vampire to be like Axel Foley from *Beverly Hills Cop*. The director was Wes Craven, and he wanted to make Freddy Krueger as a black dude. We go into the meeting with Eddie. He proceeds to tell us he wants this to be his dramatic debut. We're like, "What?" Eddie says, "I want this to be like *Shaka Zulu*." We're like, "Shaka who?" That's what we were tasked with. We went back and bridged Axel Foley, Freddy Krueger, and Shaka Zulu. (laughter) Meanwhile, we're getting pressure from the studio because we're in a race against *The Nutty Professor* at Universal—we gotta get this movie out. We wrote a script and were really happy with it. If you watch the movie, you'll see that it's a little incongruent. The president of Paramount saw the incongruency, too, and said, "You know what? We're not spending as much money on this movie as we thought." The movie's called *Vampire in Brooklyn*. I'm like, "Let's do the finale on the Brooklyn Bridge. We'll blow it up." The studio said, "No, that little scene back at Eddie's apartment, that's what the finale is going to be." They essentially cut out our third act. The movie does not end the way we envisioned because of the tonal incongruency and the financial limitations. I watched it once at the premiere in New York and never watched it again.

Michael, is there a film script that made you say, "I want to do that"?

ML: I saw *Lethal Weapon* in my senior year of college. I went and found the screenplay. Shane Black wrote this original screenplay for *Lethal Weapon* when he was a senior at UCLA. He sold it for $400,000. I'm thinking, "A hundred and twenty pages. All that blank space, some funny lines, I can do that." (laughter)

Scott, what for you was the book or poem that really sparked you to want to write?

CSW: For poetry, James Dickey was a great influence and so was John Ashbery. *Self-Portrait in a Convex Mirror* is an important text for me. *Ariadne auf Naxos* is the opera that probably meant the most to me, by Richard Strauss and the German librettist, Hugo von Hofmannsthal. And all of Wagner, as well.

What is it about writing opera that you enjoy?

CSW: Writing a libretto is essentially writing something equivalent to the book of a musical, because the libretto is the story. It's the words they sing, but it's also the dramatic movement. And of course, all my other libretti are in English. Although I have to say that a well-made opera can, in any language, communicate its essentials. It helps to know some Italian if you want to know precisely what's happening, and know Rossini, or, some of Mozart, and German, if you're wanting Wagner. But it's a highly visual medium, highly collaborative. Richard Gere's monologue in *Pretty Woman* is right when he says that you don't have to quite know exactly what they're saying in order to feel it and understand it. I feel the same way.

Give me an example. What are some words, some lines that you wrote?

CSW: The opening lines to my opera are: "It was July 4th, 1908. Or maybe it was 10,000 years ago."

I'm thinking about the conversation that you guys were having earlier about the way books are adapted to screenplays. I've been recently forced through my teenage daughter to watch a lot of musicals. What are your thoughts about how opera has evolved into this new musical thing? Like for example, Hamilton, *do you think that opera is feeding that genre? Do you think that maybe some of those older operas have adapted to musicals?*

CSW: The short answer is yes. I might say that the COVID year did change the way operas are produced, by necessity. Opera houses, opera companies, large and small, even the great Metropolitan Opera with its vast endowment, are now in a little bit of trouble, having to shut down for fifteen months. These companies operate in a very narrow margin, and in order to stay alive, almost all of them had to pivot to streaming performances. The Atlanta Opera, for instance, had to take its shows outside at Oglethorpe University, right on the soccer field, under a big tent and stream them. It was a wild ride. And it's never going to change. To be sure, as we begin to emerge from our homes and encounter each other again, people who couldn't go to concerts and be in those spaces like to be in it. That model has changed entirely.

Now, I haven't quite addressed the *Hamilton* question. I mean, are you asking whether there is a distinction between the sound of a musical and the way musicals look and feel and the way operas look and feel? Are you asking whether those two things are beginning to merge? I would say yes. Yes, for sure. There's a kind of democratization of the whole structure of who goes to the opera. In order to stay alive, it's quite possible that you won't have these stentorian baritones and tenors and these spinto sopranos anymore, that it'll just be belters who can be heard from the back seats. It'll be the Ethel Merman types who can really can just send a voice out somewhere, and maybe that will become the big selling point. I'm a little bit conservative in the sense that I don't want to see Rossini disappear. I don't want to see the classic repertory disappear simply because it's too remote and doesn't sound enough like *Grease* or *Promises, Promises* or even *Hamilton*. On the other hand, I'm all for changing and moving forward. However, I tend to work in these experimental modes anyway, so we're already weird and our audiences know it.

Reinhardt University MFA Program

NONFICTION

10 Research Topics on James Dickey's Poetry

In preparing my recent edition of James Dickey's poems,[1] I read very little criticism and attempted to confine my contributions to facts, either in terms of expanding references to real persons and events in his poems, or of citing Dickey's own comments in memoirs, articles, or interviews. Whether this latter group contains accurate information or not has been central to Dickey studies since the publication of Henry Hart's biography, but nevertheless, as they come from the author himself, they must be treated as "facts."[2]

It is no exaggeration to say that Dickey's reputation among the generation that succeeded him is, as his eldest son Christopher put it, "toxic."[3] Misbehavior at public events, insulting behavior in private, gratuitous negative criticism of his compeers in print, and most of all a decline in power and productivity from the man who was once the public face of American poetry, the inaugural poet for Jimmy Carter, singer of the Apollo moon landing, twice Poetry Consultant at the Library of Congress, a man who in a span of 14 years published 59 poems in *The New Yorker* alone.

Much came between his reputation and his poetry after 1967. The publication of *Deliverance* in 1970 assured that he would be better known for his banjo boy than for his sheep child, for the mountain men than for the Buckhead Boys. His appearances on television made him better known, in the words of Ted Koeppel, as "an American

---

1 *The Complete Poems of James Dickey*, ed. Ward Briggs (Columbia, SC: U. of South Carolina Press, 2013)
2 Henry Hart, *The World as a Lie: James Dickey* (New York: Picador, 2000).
3 In 2013 S. Tremaine Nelson, a former fiction reader at the *New Yorker*, wrote, "in the end Dickey faded from the esteem he once had enjoyed in the eyes of the literary public.""Deliverance Revisited: Its Relevance to modern American Culture is Enough to Give Alumnus James Dickey's Acclaimed Novel Another Look," *Vanderbilt Magazine* https://news.vanderbilt.edu/2020/10/29/deliverance-revisited-its-relevance-to-modern-american-culture-is-enough-to-give-alumnus-james-dickeys-acclaimed-novel-another-look/?fbclid=IwAR1-TaHDtEHjjzQDawIV-ckzEOV5_qXIN5ufhv162FFTGrSoWud556rkt5U accessed 7/21/2020.

storyteller" than as a singular poet.[4] He did not stop trying to write poetry, but he was not content to maintain the subjects, style, and metric that had won him such renown.[5] His friend Ezra Pound told him always to "make it new,"[6] or, as he used to say after reading a fine poet, "go thou and do otherwise,"[7] and he fiercely pursued that end above all in his poetry.

But in 1970 he had no great new forms to explore and no great experiences to treat beyond his increasing and debilitating reliance on alcohol (see *The Zodiac*) and a second marriage that would be considered disastrous except for the amazing daughter it produced. Ultimately, the profusion of negative stories superseded the quality of the poetry and a decade after Dickey's death, as Christopher Dickey wrote, "A mean-spirited selection of James Dickey's letters had been published. A dreary biography had appeared that claimed my father's entire world was a lie, and assumed that all the bawdy tales about him at faculty cocktail parties were the truth. After a while, I and my brother, Kevin, and our young sister, Bronwen, quit reading the stuff."[8]

It is now 25 years since his death, and over 50 since the best of his poems blazed across the literary landscape. What has become of this once-prodigious force of American poetry, anthologized in his lifetime in over sixty volumes? Today he will not be found in the *Oxford Book of American Poetry* by Lehrman and Brehm, *Good Poems* by Garrison Keillor, or Helen Vendler's *Faber Book of Contemporary Poetry*.[9] If there

---

4 *Nightline* television program, 4 July 1985.

5 Dana Gioia, "How Nice to Meet You, Mr. Dickey," *American Scholar* 72,1 (Winter 2003) reports Dickey telling him. "'I am not Dick Wilbur! I gotta grow, goddammit, I am *not* Dick Wilbur!'"

6 Pound's phrase, which he used in the introductory notes to *Ta Hio: The Great Learning, Newly Rendered into the American Language* (1928), originates in 18th-century China. See Michael North, *Novelty: A History of the New* (Chicago: U. of Chicago Press, 2013).

7 Dickey's twist on Luke 10:37 is in a letter to David Buzzard December 4, 1970, in *Crux: The Letters of James Dickey*, ed. Matthew J. Bruccoli and Judith S. Baughman (New York: Knopf, 1999) 359.

8 "The Poet's Family Album," *A Man's Journey to Simple Abundance*, ed. Sarah Ban Breathnach (Scribner, 2000)

9 *The Oxford Book of American Poetry*, ed. David Lehman and John Brehm (Oxford: Oxford University Press, 2006); *Good Poems*, ed. Garrison Keiller (New York: Penguin, 2014); *The Faber Book of Contemporary Poetry*, ed. Helen Vendler (London & Boston: Faber, 1990).

is any future need or appreciation for Dickey's poetry in anthologies to come, it will have to arise from introduction to his work in the classroom. Teachers in those classrooms will need fresh introductions to the poetry, if not the man.

Thus, the need exists for scholarly research and critical examinations of this basically accessible, universal, and engaging poetry. My greatest hope is that my new edition may help spur a renewed appreciation of Dickey by young eyes untainted by the spectacle his public persona often created. To that end, let me supply some ready topics for research usable for students seeking grades, graduate students seeking degrees, or faculty seeking tenure. Study of these aspects of Dickey's work may lead the way to a fresh appraisal of Dickey's methods, materials, and accomplishments.

Topics of Research

1. **Translation from the French:** "I read French, as well as other foreign languages, indifferently, but with the greatest excitement, and I read them all the time."[10] Dickey had first encountered his favorite French poets in Paris and at Cap d'Antibes on the French Riviera, during his *Sewanee Review* fellowship from August 1954 to June 1955. There he amassed a formidable library (now at the University of South Carolina) of mostly young French poets, especially the experimental poets of the *poésie blanche* school of men who rejected established poets like Stéphan Mallarmé (1842-98), Pierre Reverdy (1889-1960), and Arthur Rimbaud (1854-91). Such poets included André du Bouchet (1924-2001), Yves Bonnefoy (1923-2013), and René Char (1907-88).

Dickey called Louis Émié (1900-67), Lucien Becker (1911-84), and André Frénaud (1907-93), "the best poets I know."[11] In 1958, he translated poems by Bonnefoy and Becker and wrote to James Wright,

---

10 Letter to David Buzzard, 4 December 1970, *Crux*, 359.
11 *Crux*, 359. He called Becker "he best young poet writing in French today, for my money." (Crux, 138).

"American and English poets I had been reading up until a few years ago seemed to me so cautious and theory-ridden that I learned French as a relief, and for the past three years have read almost no other poets than the French."[12] In 1960, he translated Frénaud's "Les Paysans," as "The Farmers" during his son Christopher's stay in the hospital. Two years later Dickey wrote "The Owl King," employing a phrase he claimed he took from the Mauritian-born poet and dramatist Loys Masson (1915-1970).[13] Following the great critical success of *Poems 1957-1967*, Dickey searched for new forms and subjects, by which he could "make it new."

At about this time he was asked by the poet Jean Garrigue (1914-72) to contribute a translation to her edited volume, *Translations by American Poets*. Émié had recently died, and Dickey, who was still reading the French poets "all the time,"[14] produced a very careful translation of his poem, "L'Ange."[15] Nine years later Dickey produced *Head-Deep in Strange Sounds*, which contained versions of Reverdy's (1889-1960) "À quand" as "When," Léon-Paul Fargue's (1878-1947) "Voix du haut parleur" as "Low Voice, Out Loud," Alfred Jarry's (1873-1907) "L'Homme à la Hache" as "The Ax-God: Sea Pursuit," Isidore Lucien Ducasse (1846-1870), known as Comte de Lautréamont's, "chant deuxième" from *Les Chants de Maldoror* as "Math."[16]

The volume also contains poems by authors of other nationalities, some of which were translated by Dickey from French translations (See #2 below). In 1982, Dickey published *Värmland*, which contained translations of Frénaud's "Lacs du Värmland" as "Lakes of Värmland," and "Viens dans mon lit" as "Form," a poem of Becker's as "Heads," Roland Bouhéret's (1930-1995) "Pour avoir laisse les oiseaux" as "Poem [c]," and André du Bouchet's (1924-2001) "Sur le pas" as "Attempted Departure."[17] In the next year came "Craters,"

---

12 Hart, 230; *Crux*, 138.

13 The exact phrase does not occur in Masson. See *Complete*, 758.

14 *Crux*, 359.

15 "The Angel," in *Translations by American Poets*, ed. Jean Garrigue (Athens: Ohio University Press, 1970) 80-9.

16 *Head-Deep in Strange Sounds: Free-Flight Improvisations from the unEnglish* (Winston-Salem, NC: Palaemon Press, 1979).

17 *Värmland: Poems Based on Poems* (Winston-Salem, NC: Palaemon Press, 1982)

a translation from a "Chanson" by the "ex-surrealist" Michel Leiris (1901-1990).[18] Dickey's knowledge of French, by the way, remained so deep that in 1989 he conducted an entire meeting of the Alliance Française de Caroline de Sud *en Français*, reading and commenting on the French originals and his translations.

Since Dickey knew French so well and was influenced by these poets throughout his career, his translations from the French tend to show greater attention to often experimental form, meter, and diction than do his translations from other languages, and represent many of his interests in the natural world. A reader with a deep knowledge of French could describe the work of the French poets and the elements that would appeal to Dickey, assess the accuracy not only of Dickey's translations and his points of departure from the originals, but also his judgments of poets like Becker and Frénaud.

Dickey thought the original poetry of the great translator of Homer, Robert Fitzgerald (1910-85), was better than his translations and would say to him, "dig into yourself for a change, instead of into Homer and Virgil."[19] But one needs or is forced into a respite from digging. Dickey's great compeer, Robert Lowell, at about the same time published his book of translations, *Imitations*, in which he wrote, "This book was written from time to time when I was unable to do anything of my own."[20] A comparison of Dickey's books of translations with Lowell's would be useful. What poems or elements appealed to these authors at similar points in their careers? What forms or subjects from these translations appear in the poets' later work? What other poets have returned to translation during fallow periods?

2. **Translations Not from French Poets:** Despite his German heritage, Dickey claimed to have only "indifferent German."[21] In 1958, Dickey was translating French poets, but at the suggestion

18 "James Dickey with Others: Five Poems," *American Poetry Review* 12 (March/April 1983) 4;Crux, 88. For another translation of a Leiris poem, see *Crux, 88-89*
19 Letter to Robert Fagles, August 16, 1996, *Crux*, 510.
20 Robert Lowell, *Imitations* (London: Faber & Faber, 1971) xii.
21 Letter to Peter Viereck, 26 June 1980, *Crux, 391*. On his German heritage, see Hart, 4.

of James Wright, Bly sent Dickey a copy of his journal, *The Fifties*, which contained a translation of a poem by the Austrian Georg Trakl (1887-1914).[22] Bly suggested that Dickey translate some Scandinavian poets, presumably for Bly's new journal, *The Sixties*. It is not known what became of these translations, as they were never published by Bly, but Dickey began thinking about translating as his mentor Pound had done, from languages he did not know.

In 1971, he joined John Updike, Richard Wilbur, and others in "adapting" poems by Yevgeny Yevtushenko (1932-2017) for a volume called *Stolen Apples*.[23] All of the contributors to that volume made their "adaptations" from literal prose versions supplied by the publisher, beginning a pattern that Dickey would continue for the rest of his career: create a poem that was more or less faithful to an existing literal or poetic translation. To this period (1970-79) also belongs the failed free-form elaboration and improvisation on the Dutchman Hendrik Marsmann's (1899-1940) "De Dierenriem" ("The Zodiac"), which Dickey had read in translation in the *Sewanee Review* while he was a student at Vanderbilt.[24] "I have a great fondness for *The Zodiac*, because it's a failure and I knew it would be," he told Thorne Compton.[25]

He continued to render poems from other languages, almost always helped by translations, several of them in French, which he had in his library, like the poem by Italian Eugenio Montale (1896-1981) that Dickey rendered as "Nameless," that of Attila József (1905-

22 Hart, 230.
23 Dickey's contributions were: "Pitching and Rolling," "Assignation," "In Aircraft, the Newest. Inexorable Models...," "Doing the Twist on Nails," "I Dreamed I already Loved You," "Poetry Gives off Smoke," "In the Wax Museum at Hamburg," "Idol," "Old Bookkeeper," "Kamikaze," "At the Military Registration and Enlistment Center," "The Heat in Rome." *Stolen Apples with English Adaptations* by James Dickey, Geoffrey Dutton, Lawrence Ferlinghetti, Anthony Kahn, Stanley Kunitz, George Reavey, John Updike, Richard Wilbur (Garden City, NY: Doubleday, 1971). Dickey admired Yevtushenko's skill at self-promotion and hosted him at the University of South Carolina in January 1972.
24 "The Zodiac," translated by Adriaan J. Barnouw, *Sewanee Review*, 55 (Spring 1947) 238-51; James Dickey, *The Zodiac* (Garden City: Doubleday, 1976).
25 Thorne Compton, "Imagination at Full Stretch: An Interview with James Dickey," *James Dickey Newsletter* 20 (Fall 2003) 31-42.

37) that Dickey rendered as "Small Song," the Finnish Saima (Rauha Maria) Harmaja's "Poem [b]," and the Norwegian Nordahl Grieg's (1902-41) "A Saying of Farewell."[26] Dickey, like Pound, translated from the Chinese. Two versions of the same original, which Dickey called "Purgation," come from the 8th-century Chinese poet Po Chi-yi (772-846) via Witter Bynner's translation for the anthology *The Jade Mountain* (1929).

During this period, Dickey was very reliant on Pound's theories of translation and even gave a lecture on Pound (one of the few major poets on whom Dickey published) at the University of Idaho in 1979.[27] A Pound expert could find much to discuss in terms of Dickey's theory and practice relative to that of his friend. Is there evidence of Pound's theory of sound imitation in these poems and if not, why not? It would be desirable to have someone conversant with the languages and literatures of these poets closely compare Dickey's versions, published in *Head-Deep in Strange Sounds* (1979) with the originals and with the translations Dickey used in the deep way that Romy Heylen did with *The Zodiac*,[28] to understand why these poems spoke to him so forcibly.

3. **Dickey and Vicente Aleixandre:** Though Dickey did not know Spanish, he and the Mexican poet Octavio Paz (1914-1998) agreed to translate each other's poetry in 1977. Dickey obliged by translating Paz's "Vallé de Mexico" in 1978 and championed Paz for the Nobel Prize, which he won in 1990.[29] In the early 1980s, Dickey continued to produce versions from the French of Frénaud, Becker, his contemporary, André du Boucheret (1924-2001), and Leiris.[30]

---

26 "Nameless" in *Poésies (Paris; Gallimard, 1966)*; " Small Song" in *Hommage des poètes français à Attila Jozsef* (Paris: Pierre Seghers, 1955); for "Poem [b]," *Poètes finnois* (Paris: Pierre Seghers, 1951); for "A Saying of Farewell," *Poèmes choisis* (Paris: Pierre Seghers, 1954).

27 *The Water-Bug's Mittens: Ezra Pound: What We Can Use* (Bloomfield Hills, MI & Columbia, SC: Bruccoli-Clark, 1980).

28 Romy Heylen, "James Dickey's *The Zodiac*: A Self-Translation?

29 First published as a broadside by Palaemon Press in Winston Salem, then included in *Head-Deep in Strange Sounds*. Dickey reviewed Paz's *Sun Stone* in *Sewanee Review* 72 (Spring 1964) 307-21. On Dickey and Paz, see Hart, 581.

30 Frénaud: "Lakes of Värmland," "Form," & "Farmers"; Becker: "Heads"; du

But between 1982 and 1987, Dickey made versions of the (mostly very short) poems of the Spanish poet Vicente Aleixandre (1898-1984).[31] He called the process by which he made these versions "re-writing," and he "re-wrote" at least 16 of the Spanish poet's poems in this period. For all of these, Dickey relied on translations by Willis Barnstone and David Garrison in their volume *A Bird of Paper* (1982).[32] These poems are far slighter, and his translations are far less successful than his translations from the French and represent a poet of waning powers searching desperately for inspiration in the poems of others in other tongues. Why did Dickey choose these short poems and what was his special affinity with Aleixandre?

As translations became a major portion of Dickey's output (In the period 1970-79, Dickey published 34 poems, 26 of which were translations; from 1980 he published 40 original poems and 21 translations), the larger issue raised by Robert Lowell looms: These translations were published during a period when the poet's creativity was somewhat stalled and made up for his inability to make anything new. What other poets found themselves in a similar situation? The latter part of Dickey's career deserves closer analysis.

4. **Dickey and Minor Poets Who Died Prematurely:** Dickey seemed drawn to devote poems to or translate the poems of fellow poets who died young, often with an interesting backstory. Attila József threw himself under a train at age 31; the Saima Harmaja died of tuberculosis at 21; Georg Heym died at age 25 trying to save a friend who had fallen through the ice on the Elba River; and the Norwegian Nordahl Grieg was killed on a bombing mission at 41. Although Dickey was particularly harsh on nearly all of his contemporaries, he had a soft spot for poets who died relatively young. Sometimes his poems were written about the late friends of major poets he befriended.

The British poet Edward Thomas (1878-1917) died in the Battle

---

Bouhéret: "Poem [c]," "Attemtede Departure"; Leiris: "Craters."
31 He had published "Undersea Fragment in Colons" in *Head-Deep* and would publish "Circuits" in *The Eagle's Mile* (1990), for a total of 16 versions of Aleixandre.
32 He acknowledged his dependence on these translators when "World," "Earth," and "Sea" appeared in the *Kentucky Poetry Review* 20 (Fall 1984) 3-4.

of Arras in World War I at 39. Like Dickey, Thomas found his poetic talents later than most poets, but unlike Dickey, did not survive his war service. Dickey wrote "To Edward Thomas" after meeting Robert Frost (1874-1963), who called Thomas "the only human being I ever truly loved."[33] Robert Bhain Campbell (1911-40) was a very close friend of John Berryman (1914-72), with whom Dickey was initiating a friendship in 1960. Dickey called Berryman "the greatest American poet" and sent him a poem, "For Robert Bhain Campbell" about the poet's early death at 29 in 1940.

Hendrik Marsmann, author of *The Zodiac*, was trying to escape France following Hitler's invasion of the Netherlands in 1940. His ship was torpedoed, and he died at age 41. The last line of "The Strength of Fields," "My life belongs to the world. I will do what I can," comes from the Welsh poet Alun Lewis (1915-1944), who died in Burma during World War II at 29.[34] Joseph Trumbull Stickney (1874-1904), with whom Dickey conducted a "dialogue" in "Exchanges," died of a brain tumor at 30. Having come to poetry himself rather late in life, Dickey would have a special sensitivity to those who died before they could fulfill their promise. What apart from their early deaths drew Dickey to them and how does early death figure in his poems?

5. **The Movies and James Dickey's Poetry:** Among the many things that can inspire a poem, James Dickey listed "things that actually happened to you... or something you saw in a movie."[35] Films depicting the natural world have influenced a number of his poems and his poems seem to have influenced some films. According to Christopher Dickey, Walt Disney's Academy-Award-winning nature documentary, "White Wilderness," about the survival of animals in the Arctic, was a favorite of his father and one he watched with his children. A controversial (because it was not filmed in the Arctic) portion of the film depicts lemmings leaping over a cliff, but

---

33 Dickey quoting Frost in Randall A. Smith, "James Dickey Interview, Part II: November 7, 1995," *James Dickey Newsletter* 21 (Fall 2004) 39.
34 Dickey met Lewis's widow in Wales and put flowers on his grave.
35 Donald J. Greiner, "Making the Truth: James Dickey's Last Major Interview," *James Dickey Newsletter* 23 (Fall 2006) 22.

another portion of the film deals with the savagery and isolation of the wolverine, with one especially dramatic shot of the beast atop a tree.

Several elements from the movie turn up in "For the Last Wolverine" and are worth investigating. "The Heaven of Animals" was inspired by a 1955 Disney film, *The African Lion*, which documented the lives and habits of lions over a 30-month period in Uganda, Tanganyika, and Kenya. Dickey was impressed with the lions' constant need (and methods) for killing other beasts for food.[36] "The Shark's Parlor" was inspired by the 1956 film The Sharkfighters with Victor Mature. Dickey said that his poem "Adultery" was sparked by watching *Harlow* (1965), a film biography of Jean Harlow starring Carroll Baker.

We all remember Dickey's turn as Sheriff Bullard in *Deliverance* (1972), but there are curious instances in which Dickey's presence is felt in films he had nothing to do with. "A Folk-Singer of the Thirties" was written in Positano, Italy, in 1963, after Dickey had read biographies of the folksingers Woody Guthrie (1912-67) and Burl Ives (1909-95).[37] The poem involves a rail-hopping singer boarding trains and dodging railroad detectives, called "yard bulls." Dickey ends the poem with a train crossing the country with the folksinger nailed cruciform to the side of a freight car. At the end of Martin Scorsese's first big-budget film, *Boxcar Bertha* (1972), the folksinging hobo Big Bill Shelley, played by the late David Carradine, is crucified on the side of a freight car by the yard bulls. Where did Scorsese or his screenwriters, Joyce Hooper and John William Carrington, get this image?

Dickey's life (and particularly Christopher Dickey's 1998 *Summer of Deliverance*) is reflected in Tim Burton's 2003 film (but *not* Daniel Wallace's original book), *Big Fish* (2003).[38] Consider the plot: A reporter for United Press International (Billy Crudup) who is based

---

36 These films were released on DVD in 2006 with others in the "True Life" series and are readily available.

37 Woody Guthrie, *Bound for Glory* (New York: Dutton, 1943); Burl Ives, *The Wayfaring Stranger* (New York: Whittlesey Books, 1948).

38 These affinities are evident only in the film, not Daniel Wallace's novel.

in Paris, must return to a small Southern town where his father lives, from whom he has been estranged for some years, and who has told him made-up stories about a previous marriage, circus adventures, and other tall tales. The plot revolves around the son trying to separate truth from fiction in his father's stories. The father, Edward Bloom (Albert Finney), is larger-than-life, charismatic and single-minded. His much younger, beautiful wife (Jessica Lange) does not live with him anymore. Young Edward comes upon a magical village called Spectre, in which Billy Redden, the banjo player from *Deliverance*, sits on the porch of a cottage playing "Dueling Banjos."

Images from Dickey poems occur: Walking through moonlit woods, young Edward encounters a bird as in "The Owl King" or "The Lord in the Air"; a sapphire-blue swimming pool at night recalls the "blue-eyed waters" of "The Olympian" and the appearance of a naked woman in murky waters, fruitlessly pursued by the virginal young Edward, recalls "Root-Light." The film concludes with Edward's son carrying him down to the river to be carried off by the Big Fish. As they descend the riverbank, all the characters from Edward's tall tales are there to say goodbye to him. This bears a remarkable similarity to Pat Conroy's eulogy for Dickey, in which he imagines Dickey paddling a canoe past a riverbank filled with his characters.[39] There are numerous other affinities in the film and an enterprising scholar might even contact the screenwriter, John Arthur, or perhaps Tim Burton himself, who deliberately put Billy Redden in the film "for those who get it."[40] These similarities seem far more than coincidental, as opposed to simply similar themes, as in "The Sprinter's Sleep" (1957) and "Field of Dreams" (1989). How did they happen?

6. **Most Popular Poems:** *The Complete Poems of James Dickey* contains the reprint history of each poem collected. One or more of Dickey's poems appear in over 156 anthologies, listed in the apparatus criticus to the poems. Analysis of these lists will show which of Dickey's

---

39 Spoken at James Dickey's memorial service at the University of South Carolina, January 27, 1997. VHS tape available from the James Leyburn Library, Washington & Lee University, Lexington, VA 24450.
40 Tim Burton commentary on dvd of "Big Fish."

poems have been most popular with anthologists (who often borrow from other anthologists) and reveal the poems upon which the poet's identity and reputation are largely based. The most anthologized of his war poems, "The Firebombing" and "The Performance," come in at 11 and 13 reprintings respectively, comparable to the 12 reprintings of his long poem, "Falling." Why are his other great war poems like "The Driver," "Haunting the Maneuvers," "Between Two Prisoners," and "Drinking from a Helmet" not anthologized more? "Buckdancer's Choice," the title poem of his 1966 National Book Award-winning volume, is only reprinted 13 times.

The most-anthologized poems are "The Sheep Child" (21), "The Lifeguard" (26), "Cherrylog Road" (31), and "The Heaven of Animals" (32). Why are these the most popular, ranging from the shocking to the merciful? The decline in Dickey's reputation late in his life means that some fine poems published in his last years that deal touchingly with the death of his brother, his wife, and another alcoholic writer at the end of his days, do not make the anthologies or textbooks: "Last Hours," about the final illness of his brother Tom, "The Drift-Spell" about the death of his first wife Maxine, and "Entering Scott's Night," the last poem, published posthumously by *The New Yorker*, a reflection on fame and drink upon a writer of talent. Have the same poems been popular in the USA, the UK, and Europe? A comparison of the anthologized poems with the poems most discussed by critics would be a revealing picture of Dickey's reception and reputation.

7. **Multiple Sources in the Poems:** Dickey is not an allusive poet. He quotes Coleridge ("I ate the food I ne'er had eat") at the end of "Bread" and Thomas Grey in lines 85-7 of "Apollo" ("Now fades the glimmering landscape on the sight, and all the air / A solemn stillness holds"). I have recently published an article showing how Dickey's poems "The Performance," "Haunting the Maneuvers," and "The Leap" are compounded of multiple sources: personal experience, recorded history, published photographs, and the stories of others.[41] While poems like "The Bee" and "Them, Crying" reflect

---

41 "James Dickey and Life," *The Hopkins Review* n.s. 5, 2 (Spring 2012) 161-72.

actual personal experiences (in this case involving each of his sons), other poems show multiple literary influences. For instance, "The Strength of Fields" draws from Robert Frost, Virgil's *Georgics*, Arnold Van Gennep, Joseph Campbell, and Alun Lewis. "Exchanges," written for Harvard's 1970 Phi Beta Kappa ceremony, is an amalgam of lines from Harvard graduate Trumbull Stickney, the Santa Barbara Oil Spill of 1969, and an elegy to his mistress, Robin Jarecki, who died in 1967. Given Dickey's great depth of reading and his nearly photographic memory of what he read, allusions and influences are bound to appear in his work: they only need to be found.

8. **Mixed Geography in Dickey's Poetry:** Artists have no difficulty in altering the reality of a scene for artistic purposes. This was especially true among landscape painters. John Constable (1776-1837), for instance, in his 1826 painting "The Cornfield," portrays a boy and his dog herding sheep along the Fen Path, a path in woods that Constable knew intimately from his youth. Constable was meticulous in his depiction of the plants and even consulted a botanist to ensure his accuracy, but in the center background of the picture is the town's church which was nowhere near the scene in real life.

Dickey's poems also often combine geographical elements from disparate locations. "Cherrylog Road" is nominally set in Atlanta, since Dickey is reportedly meeting a belle of his high-school days, Doris Holbrook. The real junkyard was up old Georgia Route 5 near Dickey's family homestead at Mineral Bluff, Georgia. He mentions Highway 106 which runs north and south in eastern Georgia, nowhere near Atlanta or Cherry Log. The poem "Root-Light" imagines a swimmer in the St. Mary's River in Okefenokee Swamp near Florida, under the Eugene Talmadge Bridge, which is on the Georgia-South Carolina border. The J.C. Penney he sets in Folkston, Georgia, was in fact in St. Mary's. Other examples of mixed geography could be adduced and give an insight into part of Dickey's descriptive technique.

9. **James Dickey and his Family:** How consistent with reality are Dickey's portraits of close family members like his father Eugene ("Gamecock"), his mother Maibelle ("Angina," "Buckdancer's Choice," "The Voyage of the Needle"), his brother Tom (three "Sprinter" poems,

"Hunting Civil War Relics at Nimblewill Creek," "Last Hours"), his sister Maibelle and her husband ("Power and Light")? The picture of his brother-in-law is particularly negative and unrealistic. The poems of his father's illness, "The Hospital Window," "Approaching Prayer," "Gamecock," and "Sled Burial, Dream Ceremony" show the depth of Dickey's fascination with illness and fear of death.[42]

Poems like "Adultery" show his infidelity to his first wife, Maxine, while his cycle of imaginative poems purporting to illustrate aspects of his second wife Deborah shortly after their marriage are entirely fanciful and not based on any experience.[43] Dickey left a number of the *Puella* poems out of his omnibus collection, *The Whole Motion* (1992). He was told by Wesleyan University Press to save space, but did he delete poems about Deborah because of his increasing estrangement from her?[44] On the other hand, poems involving his sons Chris ("Messages," "To the Butterflies," "Them, Crying") and Kevin ("The Bee," "Giving a Son to the Sea") are based on real experiences and depict heroic and/ or joyful triumph. Family life occurs in numerous other poems (e.g., "Drums Where I Live") which deserve inspection.

10. **Poems Uncollected by James Dickey:** Dickey chose not to collect 40 poems that he published in his lifetime. Considering how many of his juvenilia and apprentice poems he chose to publish in *Veteran Birth* and *Striking In*, what distinguished these uncollected poems from the rest? In addition, a number of previously collected poems were eliminated from Dickey's summary collection *The Whole Motion* of 1992. In addition to the *Puella* poems, what did Dickey dislike about the poems omitted?

Bonus 1: **Different Poems of the Same Title:** Dickey did not alter his poems once they were published as did, for instance, W.H. Auden and Robert Penn Warren.[45] "Any subject has an infinitude of possibilities, and if I'm not satisfied with the way I did it the first time,

42 E.g., "Diabetes," "The First Morning of Cancer."
43 Mostly collected in *Puella* (Garden City, NY: Doubleday, 1982).
44 Hart, 608-9.
45 See Edward Mendelson, *Early Auden, Later Auden* (Princeton: Princeton University Press, 2017); *Selected Poems of Robert Penn Warren*, ed. John Burt (Baton Rouge, LA: Louisiana State Press, 2001) *passim*.

I just take the whole thing and start in from another angle."[46] Dickey seldom amended or altered his poems after their initial publication, but he published a small number of poems with radically revised subjects. The chief example is "Springer Mountain" written in Positano, Italy, and published in the *Virginia Quarterly Review* in 1962. The poem was almost entirely re-written and published in his volume *Helmets* in 1964.

"Under Buzzards" is the title of a poem published in the Cambridge (UK) journal *Granta* in 1963 and also a part of a poem called "Diabetes," dedicated to Robert Penn Warren. Dickey also wrote two poems called "Reincarnation" (both 1964), and he published two versions of his translation from the Chinese, "Purgation," in 1979 and a year later in 1980. The title of "Amputee Ward: Okinawa, 1945" (1948) is repeated as a tag line at the heads of "The Work of Art" (1957) and "The Contest" (1950s). "A Beginning Poet, Aged Sixty-Five" (1958) and "To Landrum Guy, Beginning to Write at Sixty" (1960) treat a similar subject. Jorge Luis Borges (1899-1986) has two poems named "Limits." What other poets have done this?

Bonus 2: **James Dickey and the Editors of *The New Yorker*:** *The New Yorker* is known for having its own stylistic rules, which authors eager to publish in its pages are happy to respect. Thanks to typescripts at Emory, we can see Dickey's original punctuation consistently altered by *The New Yorker* during Dickey's chief period of publication with them (1959-1973) and then restored by Dickey in his collections. More interesting, however, are the larger changes to the poems "Slave Quarters," "In the Child's Night," and "A Saying of Farewell." Investigation of these changes will tell a story of the magazine's editorial policy and their relationship with one of their most frequently published poets. Such a study would be enhanced by consultation of Dickey's relationships with the poetry editor during this time, Howard Moss (1922-87).[47]

Bonus 3 (for the Brave): **Dickey and Women Writers:** Dickey's

46 *The Voiced Connections of James Dickey: Interviews and Conversations*, ed. Ronald Baughman (Columbia, SC: University of South Carolina Press, 1989) 80.
47 *Crux*, 193; Hart, 235, 358, 383, 604. Moss's papers are in the Special Collections Research Center at Syracuse University.

history with women in and out of his marriages has been well documented. Notable women appear in his greatest long poems, "Falling" and "May Day Sermon." He wrote nothing about his first wife, Maxine, until he was near death. His *Puella* poems show an inability to imaginatively figure his second wife and her sister. Dickey wrote a lot of criticism which generally disprized his contemporaries, but he was particularly harsh toward female poets, whom he generally considered shallow.

In his 1976 *Paris Review* interview, Dickey spoke highly of women prose writers: "women of the South have brought into American literature a unique mixture of domesticity and grotesquerie," but that both American and British women novelists "had little breadth of experience, but much penetration into a specific and still milieu. Their scope is limited to the local and domestic with, in some cases, an admixture of the grotesque."[48] In this category he put Southern women Carson McCullers (1917-67), Eudora Welty (1909-2001), and Flannery O'Connor (1925-64). Towards prominent women poets he was less kind, especially Sylvia Plath ("She's just someone who killed herself out of literary desperation")[49] and the confessional poetry of Anne Sexton (1928-74) ("I don't care much for her either") and what he called the "scab pickers" of the "School of Abby Gabby."[50] While his negative opinions about his male peers rankled the literary world, his views on women writers made him seem a throwback. Women now write about Dickey's toxic masculinity, mostly evidenced in *Deliverance*.[51]

Ward Briggs

48 Franklin Ashley, "James Dickey: The Art of Poetry XX," *Paris Review* 65 (Spring 1976) 73-4
49 *Paris Review*, 73, where he also calls Plath "The Judy Garland of American poetry."
50 *Paris Review*, 73; "Anne Sexton," *Babel to Byzantium* (New York: Farrar, Straus and Giroux, 1968) and *Sorties* (Garden City, NY: Doubleday, 1971).
51 E.g., Sally Robinson, chapter "Damned If They Do, Damned If They Don't; *Deliverance* and the Hysterical Male Body," in *Marked Men: White Masculinity in Crisis* (New York: Columbia University Pres, 2000); Dawn B. Sova, *Literature Suppressed on Social Grounds* (New York: Facts on File, 1998) 106-8.

"Blue Iris," Gray Area: George Scarbrough and the *Bibliomenon* of Poetry

The word "so-called" in the title of George Scarbrough's 1956 book *Summer So-Called* suggests that there's a season that's commonly called "summer." It also suggests that the season's name is somehow unearned or unreliable. Extending this multivalent spirit, the book's title poem is perhaps best read by yoking the title to its first line—*"Summer so-called / My* ears, when first the stirrup galloped." This changes "so-called" to a verb instead of an adjective, as in "summer called my ears in this particular way." This reading is the only way to get the poem's rather long and complex first sentence to parse (30). I've never seen anyone else use "so-called" as a verb, and neither has the *Oxford English Dictionary*. Given Scarbrough's undisputable originality, it wouldn't surprise me if he was the first—and thus far the only—person to have done so.

As Randy Mackin documents in *George Scarbrough, Appalachian Poet*, Scarbrough loved combing his own "beloved" dictionary—"a foot thick and clumsy as a sack of grain"—for new and unusual words for his poems, which puts him in a club that counts numerous other twentieth-century poets (from the legendary Wallace Stevens to the criminally underrated Rosamund Stanhope) among its members (1). It's hardly surprising, then, that Scarbrough's poem begins with horse imagery, given that a lesser-known meaning of the word "summer" is "horizontal bearing beam," a definition derived from the Anglo-French *somier*, meaning "main beam," which is derived from the Late Latin *sagmarius*, or "pack horse." Beams of a sort are also present in the poem's first sentence, as the speaker tells of "sun- / light on the hair of [his] ears."

For me, Scarbrough's most moving poems are the ones that foreground this fusion of syntactic difficulty and linguistic play, an approach that allows language to double back on itself in order to bring forth the strangeness, complexity, and beauty of words and the world. We perhaps see the origins of this approach in "Several More Scenes from Act One," a series of prose reminiscences that first appeared in the *Appalachian Journal* in the 1970s and later republished in *New and Selected Poems*. In one scene, the poet recalls his older brother Lee handing him a "feathery dandelion," the seeds of which the young Scarbrough is unable to blow completely away (18). His brother then scoffs and says, "Let a man try," but Lee, too, is unable to rid the flower of its remaining "silvery fluff," at which point he attempts to relay to his younger brother a bit of superstitious thinking, or, in Scarbrough's words, "an unspoken message":

> "It's all right," Lee said. "Mom didn't want us anyway." He explains. "If you can blow all the seeds away, you must go on home. Your parents need you." He looks puzzled. "Or is it the other way round? If you can't blow them all away, your parents need you. I forget."

Though this is a distant memory by 1970—Scarbrough says he was three at the time, which means that the event took place more than a half century prior to his writing about it—it was clearly a formative one, as the poet's feelings about the incident make plain:

> Words, I learned early then, have this difficulty communicating, even when the speaker is sure of his fact. Their meaning becomes as stubbornly clinging or as airily escapable as the dandelion silk blown away in the wind. I remember watching the silken engines drift down, and thinking it would have been better if Lee had not mentioned his doubt—at least, not in words. Certainties are too hard to gather. He might have shrugged a shoulder, turned up a palm in a *je ne sais quoi* equivalent available even to a country boy, and the importance of his revelation to me would have remained undiminished. That way, I could have gone on rejoicing in the message and its ensorcelling way of being delivered.

But feelings made plain—or made all *too* plain—are also the root of Scarbrough's problem, and having expressed his disillusion at his brother's turning magic into mere language, he takes aim at his own musing:

> But all this commentary is rather beside the point. What I am

trying to say is that words are the least exigent in message. A hole worn in the oilcloth of a kitchen table says more about the state of my larder than a whole volume enumerating all my larder lacks. (19)

Though Scarbrough did seem to think of himself as—to use his language—a "country boy," his work is often highly learned and philosophical, at times anticipating postmodern literary criticism and at other times harking back to earlier thinkers. For instance, his attention to the concept of the trace in the scene above—in which a "a *hole* worn" in oilcloth evokes more than "a *whole* volume" (italics mine)—presages the concerns and style of certain French deconstructionists. Scarbrough's dialectical take on the specter of language recalls Karl Marx, who, as Fredric Jameson puts it:

> urges us to do the impossible, namely, to think . . . positively and negatively all at once; to achieve, in other words, a type of thinking that would be capable of grasping the demonstrably baleful features of capitalism along with its extraordinary and liberating dynamism simultaneously within a single thought. (47)

If I may take the liberty of replacing the word "capitalism" with the word "language" and the words "human race" with the word "poet" in the sentence of Jameson's that immediately follows the one just quoted, I think there are times when Scarbrough allows us "to lift our minds to a point at which it is possible to understand that [language] is at one and the same time the best thing that has ever happened to the [poet], and the worst."

Being a poet—and I daresay it often feels to me like he's all *poet*—Scarbrough is beholden to and invested in language in a particularly intense way. He's also honest about his fraught attitude toward his materials, in that he plainly acknowledges language's insufficiency even as he harnesses its great power. Elsewhere in "Several More Scenes from Act One," he refers to himself as "a man who has given up, or is giving up, all attempts at communication with his neighbors" and claims that "words helped to make [him] a loner." At the same time, he's left his readers many difficult, rigorous, and stunning poems, several of which put the problem with words *into* words in a rather dynamic way (*New and Selected Poems* 17, 19).

One such poem is "Blue Iris," also from *Summer So-Called*, in which we might hear a bit of Vincent Van Gogh's notion of being "haunted by the idea that the convention of painting prevented him from seizing the reality before him" (Ross 84). Here's the first of the poem's three stanzas:

> To subjugate a quality to a principle
> Of containment not necessarily contained
> In nature, is to describe the iris:
> Before the storm, a fine light rained
> Itself to atoms on the heated ground
> Until about the iris roots was saturate
> With yellowbronze, yellowbronze
> That must spill upward or be satiate
> Under blue out-riders nimbus-whorled
> With light's too multitudinous fiery state! (83)

This opening perhaps sounds more like a sentence from Edmund Husserl's *Origin of Geometry* than a lyric poem, but when we arrive at the word "iris," we find ourselves in more familiar territory, not only with regard to poetry in general, which of course regularly takes up the subject of flowers, but also regarding Scarbrough's poems in particular, many of which use flowers as a point of departure for thinking about thinking. To further explore Scarbrough's flower poems beyond "Blue Iris," I suggest "Tropic of Cancer," "Small After-Church Poem," and "Iris," all from the second section of his *New and Selected Poems*.

Before he gets to the word "describe," Scarbrough's speaker describes the act of describing, which he says renders "a quality" of a natural object—in this case, an iris—subordinate to words, which are "not necessarily contained / in nature." The poem's second line contains the word "contain" twice, first in the word "containment," by which the speaker clearly means "control" or "suppression," and then again in the word "contained," by which the speaker clearly means "included." In addition to marking the poem's third moment of repetition—the first two being repetitions of the words "to" and "a"—the word "contained" also sets up the poem's first rhyme, which we hear two lines later with "rained." In each of the poem's three ten-line stanzas, all of the even-numbered lines contain rhymed words—lines two and four with one rhyme, lines six, eight, and ten with another—while the odd-numbered lines do not rhyme.

This rhyme scheme eventually leads to "no," "know," and "so" in the final stanza, a sonic portrait of the poem in miniature and an echo of "the daily rhymes of a mountain child" (*New and Selected Poems* 19). Likewise, the describing of description will be revisited in the poem's last stanza, but in the meantime, we bear witness to the speaker "practicing / description" of the iris, which begins with the sun shining on and around the flower prior to an afternoon storm. A "yellowbronze" light saturates the ground and roots below the iris, which in turn causes nutrients to "spill upward" into it. The petals are described as "blue out-riders nimbus-whorled / With light's too multitudinous fiery state," which brings a change in the weather:

> Rain in reverse of gold swimming the flower,
> Itself hot concentrate of morning air
> Bluer than April virus entering the blood
> Of the world, rippled by thunder blare
> In the rising dazzle of noon and terse heat
> Over the contracting, inner road of storm!
> Smiled at by crooked teeth of violence
> And mouths of whirlpool yellow, the blue form
> Of flower sinks to vortices of gusts, rain
> Cools the troubled mind whose sense grows warm,
>
> Hot with the possibility of fraud
> In the blue flower, engulfed, less than a shard
> Of blue now that the world has come
> Like a gray bird walking in a close yard
> Mountained with rain.

The second stanza presents us with the curious phrase, "Rain in reverse of gold swimming the flower," which I take to mean that the storm has now filled the iris with rain, a "reverse" saturation in that the flower is now covered with cool liquid rather than bathed in warm light. In the face of the storm—or, as Scarbrough writes, the "thunder blare," the "crooked teeth of violence" and the "vortices of gusts"—the flower "sinks," a movement opposite noon's "rising dazzle," and as the poem moves from its middle stanza to its third, the rain begins to "cool" the speaker's "troubled mind," even as its "sense grows warm, // Hot with the possibility of fraud / In the blue flower."

But what is this "fraud"? Are we now in the presence of a "so-called" iris? Halfway through the third stanza, the speaker turns his attention back to his own meaning-making activity, observing that even as his mind clings to the memory of the sun-soaked iris, the flower has been rendered "less than a shard / of blue" by the dark of the storm. The poem's last sentence is devoted to describing writing, the "principle of containment" of the first stanza:

> All is maximum gray,
> Position lost in a world in which no
> Position is assured: and practicing
> Description lest my memory fail, I know,
> Chameleon that I am, because its word is there,
> The iris is not necessarily so.

The speaker's final metaphor is devoted to himself—he's now a "chameleon," a word that contains "am," the first-person, present-tense conjugation of the verb "to be." His change of subject coincides with his own change of color—a color akin, perhaps, to a pencil's graphite—as he blends in with the gray that's come to mute the iris's bluer-than-April-virus blue.

Having initially oriented himself in the world with help of the iris, the speaker is now adrift, positionless, but his describing has conferred new knowledge upon him. Echoing both its own second line and a famous Gershwin line about not believing everything you read ("The things that you're liable / To read in the Bible / It ain't necessarily so") the poem ends with the speaker coming to "know . . . the iris is not necessarily so." But "so" *what*, exactly? I take Scarbrough's "so" to mean that the iris is not necessarily "there" for him in the way that "its word" now is. In order to recall and retain his vision of the iris, the speaker has "practice[ed] / description" of it, but in doing so, he's replaced the flower's phenomena with the words of his poem, just as the storm's "maximum gray" has erased those same qualities.

Examining the "body of written science" in his book *L'Activité Rationaliste de la Physique Contemporaine*, Gaston Bachelard, who wrote extensively on both poetics and the philosophy of science, notes that:

> this body of thought in print is well suited to emphasize the adherence of scientific thought to the special language of science, to the language created as scientific discoveries are being made. It only takes a moment of reflection to recognize that this language isn't natural. (7)

Scarbrough's poem begins with a similar assumption with regard to lyric poetry. For Bachelard, "the noumena of scientific thought are tools of thought," a notion that recalls Coleridge's "Frost at Midnight," in which the speaker observes that a film of soot "flutter[ing] on the grate" of his fireplace possesses "dim sympathies" with him:

> Making it a companionable form,
> Whose puny flaps and freaks the idling Spirit
> By its own moods interprets, every where
> Echo or mirror seeking of itself,
> And makes a toy of Thought. (168-9)

If "the noumena of scientific thought are tools," then the noumena of poetic thought are perhaps more like *toys*, and yet both can be said to "shed light on . . . syntax" (Bachelard 7). "The philosopher speaks of phenomena and noumena," writes Bachelard, "Why wouldn't he give his attention to the being of the book, to the *bibliomenon*?" (6). In his beautiful and bewildering "Blue Iris"—written a decade prior to Jacques Derrida's "Structure, Sign, and Play in the Discourse of the Human Sciences," but also nearly a century after Emily Dickinson's poem 1017 ("Perception of an object costs / Precise the Object's loss")—George Scarbrough does exactly, and exactingly, that.

Thanks to my colleague Lindsay Turner for her help with my translation of the Bachelard excerpts, and to the Faculty Senate and the College of Arts Humanities and Social Sciences at the University of Denver for the sabbatical that helped me to write this and other essays.

Graham Foust

Works Cited

Bachelard, Gaston. *L'Activité Rationaliste de la Physique Contemporaine* 2nd ed., Presses Universitaires du France, 1965.

Coleridge, Samuel Taylor. *Selected Poems*, edited by William Empson and David Pirie, Carcanet, 1989.

Jameson, Fredric. *Postmodernism, or The Cultural Logic of Late Capitalism*. Duke UP, 1991.

Mackin, Randy. *George Scarbrough, Appalachian Poet: A Biographical and Literary Study with Unpublished Writings (Contributions to Southern Appalachian Studies)*, vol. 29, McFarland, 2011.

Ross, Alex. *The Rest is Noise: Listening to the Twentieth Century.* Picador, 2007.

Scarbrough, George. *New and Selected Poems.* Iris Press, 1977.
---. *Summer So-Called.* E.P. Dutton and Company, 1956.

Forty Years after *A Confederacy of Dunces*

When a true genius appears in the world, you may know him
by this sign: that the dunces are all in confederacy against
him. –Jonathan Swift

In 1979, I moved to Baton Rouge, Louisiana, from Austin, Texas, to take a position at Louisiana State University Press—the year before *A Confederacy of Dunces* was released to great acclaim. The book has the distinction of being the first novel published by a university press to win the Pulitzer Prize for Fiction and the first Pulitzer Prize awarded to a posthumous author. The story of its publication and the backstory of John Kennedy Toole—already dead from suicide at the age of thirty-one when the book was finally released—make it noteworthy in publishing history.

John Kennedy Toole wrote *A Confederacy of Dunces* in the early 1960s while he was serving in the army in Puerto Rico and teaching English as a second language to Spanish-speaking recruits. Before being drafted, he had graduated from Tulane University, received an MA in English from Columbia University, and taught at the University of Southwestern Louisiana and Hunter College. After his army service, he taught at Dominican College in New Orleans. He wrote an earlier novel, *The Neon Bible*, when he was only sixteen. Grove Press published *The Neon Bible* in 1989 amid a controversy with Toole's heirs, who refused to give up their rights to the manuscript as they had with *A Confederacy of Dunces*. As a result, his mother, Thelma Toole, would not allow the book to be published if the relatives were going to share the profits. After her death, Toole's relatives filed a lawsuit and the book was released for publication but never to the acclaim that *A Confederacy of Dunces* received. Toole had also worked on another book, *The Conqueror Worm*, but nothing ever came of it.

A Confederacy of Dunces is centered around the character Ignatius Reilly, an obese, lazy medievalist who hates work and modern society.

The book takes place in New Orleans and follows Ignatius through several menial jobs. At one point he pushes a Lucky Dog hot dog cart through the French Quarter, while another job involves working for Levy Pants where his filing method consists of tossing papers into a trash can rather than filing them. He has digestive problems and is focused on his pyloric valve, which responds in prophetic ways to the modern world. Toole's characters are eccentric, as he captures the New Orleans scenery and dialect in a humorous yet realistic way.

In February 1964, Toole attempted to publish his manuscript and entered a two-year correspondence with Simon & Schuster editor Robert Gottlieb. By Christmas, Toole received a response from Gottlieb, complimenting him on the manuscript but with suggested revisions. In March 1965, Toole responded to Gottlieb that he did not want to change the characters, who were based on real people. He then followed up with an unsuccessful visit to New York to talk with Gottlieb in person; however, he was out of the office when Toole arrived. They talked by phone after his visit, and again, Gottlieb encouraged him but insisted the manuscript needed work and suggested Toole begin a new project. Toole wrote to Gottlieb, saying he would not change the book and asked for the return of his manuscript. Later, his mother encouraged him to take the manuscript to a visiting professor at Tulane, Hodding Carter, Jr., who complimented him on the work but did not show much interest. This incident embarrassed Toole, which threw him into a state of depression and paranoia, as well as infuriated him that his mother would place him in such a situation to be rejected face to face.

In the fall of 1968, after entering Tulane with the intention of earning his Ph.D., Toole's mental decline continued until he was unable to work. He took a leave of absence from his teaching job at Dominican and incompletes in his courses at Tulane. He then began drinking heavily, gained weight, and became disheveled, a distinct change from his usual dapper appearance. After Christmas, he had a fight with his mother about his lack of employment, withdrew money from his bank account, and drove to California where he visited the Hearst Castle. On the way back to New Orleans, he ended his life.

After Toole's death, Thelma found a dog-eared carbon copy of the manuscript on top of her son's armoire and set out to see it through to publication. She was so convinced of the literary merits of the manuscript, she sent it to seven other publishers; however, she was met with no success, as most editors thought the manuscript was too regional in its subject matter and feared it had no sales potential. Thelma Toole had heard that famed author of *The Moviegoer*, Walker Percy, was teaching English at Loyola University that semester and tried to reach him by telephone and by letters, but to no avail. Finally, Thelma showed up at his office and insisted he read her son's novel. Unable to avoid her dogged persistence, Percy read the manuscript and was amazed at how good it was. At first, Percy sent the manuscript to his own publisher, Farrar, Straus and Giroux, who turned it down. He then sent it to LSU Press.

Percy met with press director Les Phillabaum, who was enthusiastic about the book. The press had begun a program of publishing literary fiction, and its reviewers found *A Confederacy of Dunces* to be worthy of publication. In addition, the Loyola University literary journal, *The New Orleans Review*, recognized its literary merits, and in July 1978, published excerpts of the manuscript. The editor of the journal at that time was Dawson Gaillard, who was a friend of Walker Percy and was working as advertising manager at LSU Press while on sabbatical from her teaching job at Loyola. While at LSU Press, she wrote marketing copy, including many of the ads and press releases for Toole's book.

In his evaluation of the book for the faculty advisory committee of LSU Press that stamps a final approval for all books published by the press, Percy wrote:

> John Toole's novel, *A Confederacy of Dunces*, is, I can say without hesitation, a fantastic novel, a major achievement, a huge comic-satiric-tragic one-of-a-

kind rendering of life in New Orleans. No one has ever or ever will capture the particularity of the backstreets, middle-and lower-class whites, blacks, and other ethnics as Toole has.

I have never come across a novel in manuscript which has impressed me as this one has.

Percy also wrote the foreword to the published book and described his dread about reading the manuscript when Thelma first presented it, but then how pleasantly surprised he was at its contents. He was impressed by the descriptions of New Orleans, its neighborhoods, and unique dialects of the white and black residents of the city. He noted that:

> Toole's greatest achievement is Ignatius Reilly, himself, intellectual, ideologue, deadbeat, goof-off, glutton, who should repel the reader with his gargantuan bloats, his thunderous contempt and one-man war against everybody—Freud, homosexuals, heterosexuals, Protestants, and the assorted excesses of modern times.

At LSU Press in the fall of 1979, the manuscript for *A Confederacy of Dunces* was already in hand in the LSU Press offices. When I arrived in Baton Rouge to work at the press, I could tell something important was happening. When a hot manuscript, such as *A Confederacy of Dunces*, is in a publishing house, you can sense the buzz in the air. Excitement about the work moved through the editorial department to production and marketing. Martha Lacy Hall, who would later retire in 1984, was the editor of Toole's book and an accomplished writer herself. She shepherded it through the process with minimal editing and revision.

The previous production/design manager, Dwight Agner, had already designed the book, and I was there to follow it through the typesetting, proofreading, and printing stages, as well as design the dust jacket. I commissioned the cover illustration to Ed Lindlof, who wrote to Thelma that "I am especially pleased . . . to hear that you are happy with the cover art for the book" after she sent him candy and note cards in thanks for his illustration. Just as some manuscripts have a dark cloud over them and everything seems to go wrong in publication, from author discontent to design and distribution, Toole's novel was the antithesis. As the manuscript moved through publication, staff members from the business office and clerical staff not directly involved in the editorial, production, or marketing process wanted to read galleys to find out what the excitement was about.

Most scholarly books published by university presses receive little attention other than reviews in academic journals, so when the mainstream prepublication reviews started pouring in, our instinct about the book was confirmed. For instance, in the March 1980, *Kirkus Review* called *A Confederacy of Dunces* "brilliant, relentless, delicious, perhaps even classic. Unfortunately, this is all we have of Toole's talent; he committed suicide in 1969, age 32, leaving only this astounding book." The April 11, 1980 review in *Publisher's Weekly* notes that the way the author "crams invention and exuberance into a perversely logical plot and molds his Pandora's box of ills into a comic novel which rings with laughter is something of a miracle." A later review in the *Washington Post* called it "a gross farce, a blustering satire, an epic comedy, a rumbling, roaring avalanche of a book that begins with a solitary fat man but quickly picks up cops and B-girls, clerks and capitalists, most of the deviates and degenerates of the French Quarter of New Orleans and keeps right on gathering momentum until it sweeps away everything, including that most innocent of bystanders, the reader, in its path."

Although university presses specialize in publishing scholarly works, a few have fiction and poetry programs to publish works of value that have been ignored by larger commercial houses. Manuscript reviewers found that Toole's regional descriptions and unique voice made a contribution to the literature of the area and recommended publication based on its merits, not on its projected income, a factor important for most commercial houses. In fact, *A Confederacy of Dunces* was originally published with the help of a grant from the National Endowment of the Arts to help cover its publication costs as it was not expected to recoup expenses. As the reviews and advance sales poured in, the original print run was increased from 1,500 copies to 2,500 copies in anticipation of its success. Another 6,000 copies were printed before publication because the advance sales already exceeded the number of books printed.

The primary mission of scholarly publishing, such as at LSU Press, is "to advance knowledge," to publish books, make them available, and provide an academic contribution but not necessarily for a profit. This altruistic purpose of scholarly publishing appealed to me, as I found it exciting to work on a project such as *A Confederacy of Dunces*, especially since it went unnoticed by so many others beyond the academic community. I loved this focus and the many aspects of the process—editorial, production, design, marketing, subsidiary rights, sales, and distribution. I had worked in scholarly publishing since the early seventies, moving from production assistant at The University of North Carolina Press to assistant production manager at the University of Texas Press to production/design manager at Louisiana State University Press—a normal progression for a young, unencumbered, publishing professional. To work firsthand on a book such as *A Confederacy of Dunces* was not the norm, however. The humor, regional flavor, and commercial interest were a sharp contrast to more serious scholarly works that were usually published by university presses.

Moving to Baton Rouge was a shock. I had been living in Austin, Texas, where the sky was wide open and higher than any I'd ever seen. The 1960s were still in bloom in Austin—blues on 6th Street, ashrams in the neighborhoods, the nudist Hippy Hollow on Lake Travis. I left UT Press mainly because of the politics that flew in like a Blue Norther that took you by surprise. I met with director Les Phillabaum and executive editor Beverly Jarrett at a meeting of the Association of American University Presses that summer and was invited to Baton Rouge for a second interview.

Baton Rouge was different from the wide open and *anything's possible* environment of Texas. Back then, few people there ate whole wheat bread, bean sprouts, or vegetarian food, all of which were staples for me. Instead, I discovered Oysters Bienville, jambalaya, and beignets. When I interviewed for the job at LSU Press and visited Baton Rouge during the summer, I marveled at steam rising from the ground that morning as I exited the Faculty Club, adding to the shadows and nuances of the place. I moved that fall, excited by the promotion and opportunity to work for such an esteemed regional publisher.

The city was family-oriented and staid, sitting below the Mississippi River that was held up by levees. The seafood, music, and Cajun accents added a charm that was slower to access but much calmer than the hip Austin. Live oak trees dripping with Spanish moss and overwhelming humidity added flavor to the gumbo of the place, particularly when I visited Dohn Barham, the business manager, and his wife in Plaquemines Parish, just down the river from Baton Rouge where they were restoring an old plantation. We took long rides along the bayous and enjoyed the swampy scenery and crawfish boils along the way.

The offices at LSU Press were in an old classroom building on the university campus waiting for the renovation of the French House that was previously a French-speaking dormitory but was promised to the press as its new home. As department manager, I sat in the middle office between the receptionist and designers. Salesmen usually assumed I was the secretary since I was a young female. Bank tellers told me they had never met a woman who had moved somewhere just for a job and asked what family I had in the area. Most of the staff at LSU Press were from the area, but some of the managers had come from other presses, such as Bob Summers, marketing manager, who previously worked at UNC Press when I was there, and Dohn Barham, who had come from Texas.

When I was working at the University of Texas Press, before coming to LSU, we experienced the excitement of having a book on *The New York Times* bestseller list. One of the acquisition editors, Archer Mayor, found the sequel to *A Once and Future King*, titled *The Book of Merlyn*, in the archives of the Harry Ransom Center. No one had noticed that it was a T.H. White unpublished manuscript because it was catalogued under the subject of "marlin fishing." The UT Press published the book in 1977. The place felt like it was floating on air as we marveled about the newspaper articles and media exposure, as well as sales, this phenomenon brought—and lots more work for the production and distribution side. We were ordering reprints of 20,000 copies every two weeks to keep up with demand. Although this experience was common for big New York publisers, it was a rare occurrence for regional university presses. Since I had been working in production at Texas as we ordered reprints, I was not completely surprised by the printing demands when I got to LSU Press.

The orders for *Confederacy* kept pouring in, so the production department at LSU Press was challenged with ordering fast reprints to keep up with the demand. More favorable reviews appeared in newspapers across the country and sales continued to increase. LSU's purchasing office insisted on a more bureaucratic approach to printing than at the University of Texas. The production office had to submit six copies of multi-page documents with specifications and comparative printing bids to the purchasing office and then wait weeks for approval before we could order more books. Since we had to go back to press more quickly than for a normal reprint, I had to appeal to a university official for a special dispensation to order printing quickly to keep up with the runaway success. Combined sales of the hardback and paperback books totaled over one million and a half copies, and sales continue to this day.

One of the challenges with runaway bestsellers is when and how to order reprints. Since a return policy exists in book publishing that allows bookstores to return unsold books, it is always a gamble for a publisher to determine how many to print and how many to anticipate will be returned. At Texas, the last reprint of 20,000 copies of *The Book of Merlyn* exceeded demand and the returns almost wiped out all the earnings. At LSU, we were more modest in the reprints and did not suffer such large returns.

Although the hardback did not make *The New York Times* bestseller list, it was on the local bestseller list in *The Washington Post*, *The Philadelphia Inquirer*, and the *Chicago Tribune*. The paperback rights were purchased by Grove Press for $2,000 before the rave reviews were in, which resulted in a first printing of 500,000, and that edition made *The New York Times* bestseller list in 1981. In addition, the book was a Book-of-the-Month Club selection and translated into twenty-two languages, including Danish, French, German, Spanish, Swedish, Norwegian, Portuguese, and Finnish. Audio rights were sold to Dove Books on Tape. The press was anxious with anticipation when Diane Guidry, the subsidiary rights manager, conducted a bidding war for the movie rights, which were bought by producer Scott Kramer and backed by Johnny Carson Movie Productions, although the movie has never been brought to fruition. She entertained more offers for translations, and more special sales occurred during that time than in all the history of the press previously. The sales, the excitement, and the media attention changed the pulse of the place as each new day unfolded. Guidry notes that "It was especially interesting to me to see all the book jacket interpretations from the foreign rights publications from all the different countries. It was a cold, wintery day in New York when I met with Grove Press regarding the sale of the paperback rights. But one that certainly turned into a sunny, exciting experience for all of us at the LSU Press."

Excitement about the book continued that year as we struggled to keep up with the printing demands. The marketing department placed ads in major publications and press releases went out to update the news of translations and sales. Soon after publication, a launch party and book signing event was scheduled at Maple Street's Garden District Book Shop in New Orleans on April 24, 1980, with Thelma Toole and Walker Percy in attendance to sign books in place of the deceased author. As part of the entertainment, Thelma had a piano brought in so she could entertain the guests with her music. Rolling her *r's* and explaining how she had taught theater and elocution for many years, she played the piano and sang, basking in the attention. She played the piano well and her songs were shrill and over-punctuated as she sought to command attention of the crowd over the background noise of the gathering. The reception included wine and hors d'oeuvres, which I enjoyed while talking with Walker Percy.

"I've never been to a book signing with such entertainment, have you?" I asked him, smiling while listening to the dramatic presentation. He nodded in amusement as the room was held captive by Thelma's singing and piano playing, although we were not paying close attention to her performance but enjoyed the refreshments.

As Percy and I continued laughing and generally goofing around, Mrs. Toole stopped playing. She turned her attention our way and admonished us with the statement, "I may not make *great* music, but I do make good music." In other words, shut up and listen to me.

Some people saw her as pretentious, bossy, and overly dramatic as she idealized her son and praised his intelligence and talent. She considered herself cultured and raised her son to be the same. To her, he was the epitome of elegance, grace, and education. He was, in fact, a brilliant student, teacher, and raconteur. However, his mother's overbearing personality was a constant source of strife in his life with her exaggerated sense of importance. Although living a middle-class existence, she had visions of grandeur about herself that she projected onto her son. While most people thought Toole modeled his character Ignatius Reilly after either his medievalist friend, Bobby Byrne, or himself, some think he was parodying his mother.

Her sense of self-importance came through at the book signing event and later at a musical theatre production written by Frank

Galati, drama professor at Northwestern University, sponsored by the LSU Theatre department. In a review in *Enterprise* (High Point, NC), Galati said, "The characters in the book are even revolting and Ignatius can be hideous, mean spirited, and even cruel. But at the same time, there is a tremendous amount of energy in the characters."

Mrs. Toole attended the opening on February 24, 1984, and she made a grand entrance. I was in attendance as she strolled down the aisle with the help of her walker, waving to the crowd like a queen, basking in the adulation that her son's work had generated. "This has been a beautiful evening in the American theater," Thelma said on opening night after the production. She was later flown to New York for interviews and seemed to enjoy all the attention that the book generated.

People wonder why Toole took his own life. He was brilliant, skipped two grades in elementary school, and received scholarships to well-known universities. He was liked among his classmates and known for his humor and wit. Very dapper as a young man, only toward the end of his life did he become disheveled and depressed. Was it his lack of success at being published that pushed him over the edge or underlying emotional problems, or both?

His relationship with his mother, who put him on a pedestal, was complicated. She felt she had married beneath her station—her husband was a used-car salesman from an Irish family, not French as her ancestors were. Most likely she projected all of her hopes and dreams onto her only child, who was cultured, intelligent, attractive, as well as conflicted. When Thelma married, she had to quit teaching in the public schools, as was the custom of the time. After that, she taught piano and elocution from her home. This must have been frustrating for a talented young woman who seems to have lived her life through the achievements of her son, a difficult situation for both parties. While Kenny, as he was called, may have inherited some emotional instability from his father who suffered from paranoia and dementia later in life, the young man's social life is a mystery.

Although he had numerous female friends, none ever became more than casual dates. We can speculate on the cause of his mental decline based on the publishing facts and his relationship with his mother but will probably never know exactly what battles he was fighting. Whatever triggered his breakdown, we get a glimpse of how clever and funny he was with his sharp wit and eye for dialogue, character, and place that come through *A Confederacy of Dunces*.

In 1969, Toole embarked on a trip around the country in his car, visiting California and the Hearst Castle called La Cuesta Encantada (The Enchanted Hill) in San Simeon. He also attempted to visit Flannery O'Connor's farm, Andalusia, in Milledgeville, Georgia; however, it wasn't open to the public at the time. On the return, instead of completing his trip in New Orleans, Toole stopped in Biloxi, Mississippi, about seventy-five miles east of The Big Easy. He left a suicide note in an envelope in the car. The letter was turned over to his mother; however, she destroyed it without revealing its contents. Later, she provided contradictory accounts of what was in the note. It has been speculated that Toole simply could not fathom returning home to his overbearing mother and he could not accept his failure to get his manuscript published. On March 26, 1969, Toole connected a garden hose from the exhaust pipe of his car to the window and killed himself. He was buried at Greenwood Cemetery in New Orleans.

Joanna Hill

Embracing the "Spirit of the Unknown and Unknowable": Private Marion (James Dickey, Some of the Time)

> *"Dickey has not been interested in communion with other humans through acceptance of the human condition but in getting beyond ordinary humanity to participate in the life of nonhuman creatures and more-than-human forces . . . His concern is not the limitations but the possibilities of human and nonhuman nature, not history but vision."*
>
> Monroe Spears

A few weeks before his journey took him to the undiscovered country, I drove to Columbia, South Carolina, for what turned out to be my last visit with Jim Dickey—*before* he died. Surrounded by bastions of his beloved books, he sat in his big chair that afternoon and read to me from the new novel. As was our ritual, I reported on how the fish were biting in Bluffton and what new birds I'd seen, turning to them in the field guide while he asked what I thought of their colors and sounds, the patterns of their flight. When it was time to leave, he took my right hand in his, opened my fingers out, and gently kissed the palm of my hand. Then he rolled my fingers into a fist, around which he held his own hands and said, "Now you hold on tight to that and can't nothin' bad ever happen to you."

And so, I have held on tight to that blessing, an abiding treasure of my life that has amplified through the years into wonderfully serendipitous experiences, including the one that inspired the brief poem, "Visitant." The genesis of that final well-wish was the first day of my first semester with him, when he began the course pretty much the same way he opened the last creative writing class of his life on January 14, 1997—five days before his death— "This is going to take us through some very strange fields, across a lot of rivers, oceans, mountains, forests. God knows where it will take us. That is part of the excitement of it, and the sense of deep adventure. Which is what we want more than anything. Discovery. Everything is in that. Everything *is* that" (Dickey 281).

I surely discovered a very great deal in those seven years that James Dickey was my teacher, friend, and mentor. He was Graduate Director for my MFA in Creative Writing, then co-director, with Don Greiner, for my Ph.D. (until he up and died on us, leaving Dr. Greiner and me both in the lurch). I'd been out of college for eight years when I began my MFA, working as a museum curator, then with a small weekly newspaper, when life offered me the chance to "change up" and I was heading to law school—like my father, my sister, my brother. It had really cooked my daddy's grits that I didn't follow in his footsteps like my younger siblings, and finally I had the chance to redeem myself. But then, much to the chagrin of dear old dad, I came to the realization that what I *really* wanted to do was write, creatively.

In the spring semester of 1990, I first walked into James Dickey's classroom—on January 16—my birthday. Auspicious indeed. One of those days in one's experience that mark real change. And change my world he did. His validation of the creative life and his insistence on a balance between the thinking self and the instinctive "creature-self" resonated through the fibers of my being. This was a mindset with which I had no familiarity—something I never knew with my own father, the ever-rational attorney.

And yes, Dickey was something of a father figure to me, one who counseled and encouraged and taught me—about writing, about humanity, and about how you can't be fully engaged in a life of the mind unless you also get your hands dirty and live in the physical world. He taught me in the classroom and during our walks through the Horseshoe (the big green space on the USC campus), during visits at his home or mine, in conversations under a canopy of trees or at the McCutchen House faculty lounge. Early on, my dear mother feared some Svengali scenario, but she needn't have worried. Dickey struck many a chord of my sensibilities, but I was never spell-bound in that way. In part, because he reminded me of my own imposing father, I wasn't intimidated by his "largeness." I think he liked that. I think it's part of what made us pals.

In those years that I was under his wing, I witnessed various facets of Dickey's world, and I am abundantly aware of his excesses and imperfections and archaic attitudes—the outdated outlook of a white Southern male who "came up," as my own father did, during the earlier decades of the last century. I know the tales, and I knew the profoundly complex man behind the persona. As is the nature of personas, much of his was bluff. Just like my own father, Dickey loved to "mess with" people, to "get a rise" out of people, to leave them, if not offended outright, then at least uncertain of exactly what to think. It's a kind of "fun" that isn't for everybody, that is for certain, and many were not amused by Dickey's imp of the perverse.

Incorporated into his persona were an assortment of demons, mixed with a big dose of bravado. Beyond that persona was far more—Private Marion, for example. In conversation one day we had lit into the topic of movies—favorite films, favorite actors, favorite roles. He told me of a little-known World War II movie entitled *The Eve of St. Mark* wherein Vincent Price plays a newly-minted Southern soldier serving in the South Pacific, a rather cynical but well-heeled poetry-quoting fellow with a fondness for the bottle. His name is Private Marion—Private Francis Marion, that is, descended from the revered Revolutionary War hero known as the Swamp Fox. Vincent Price isn't the star of the movie, but the character he portrays affected Dickey deeply.

During the crescendo of the film, Private Marion rises above himself to inspire his platoon with valor that is sincere and non-bombastic. When Dickey remarked that this was the character to whom he felt most deeply connected and by whom he was most inspired, I took to calling him Private Marion. I'm not sure exactly when this began, but the inscription in my copy of *The Whole Motion* reads, "To The Other Wonder—from Private Marion (James Dickey, some of the time)—Fall, 1992—." His nickname for me was "The Other Wonder," from a poem I'd written in his class.

Chris Dickey knew nothing of the film or his father's affinity for Private Marion and was fascinated when I shared the story with him during a James Dickey Colloquium that took place in 2017. I will always be grateful to the folks at Reinhardt University who organized the conference that provided Chris and me with ample time for heart-to-heart talks about Big Jim while we were housemates for a few days on campus. So many stories, painful and joyful—but never mundane.

For Dickey, nothing was worse than boring. He liked to quote the advice he attributed to the French writer Henry de Montherlant—"If your life ever begins to bore you, risk it." That risk included forays into shadowy, dangerous places in Dickey's life and in his writing. *To the White Sea* is the novel he was working on during my tenure with him, and it is dark indeed. Thrilling and dark. When you find yourself pulling for a full-fledged sociopath, war or no war, it makes you squirm. Then, of course, there is *Deliverance*—not to mention the myriad places of discomfort to which much of his poetry takes us. He taught each of us who came under his tutelage that a writer must have guts enough to dance with the dark side that is part of everyone's makeup, to explore those nether regions of self that we suppress at Sunday School and Junior League.

Yet Dickey was also capable of childlike glee, in his work and in his life—fun for the glorification of fun. I think of the afternoon we were walking across the Horseshoe, surrounded by stately old buildings and filled with grand old trees. A gorgeous spring day, everything in bloom.

He said, "Wouldn't it be wonderful to lie there in that thick grass and look up at the clouds?"

"Yes," I said.

"Well, come on," he said, "let's do it."

"Do you really think we should?" I asked.

"Why not?" was his question.

A very valid question. So we did. We lay there like little kids and laughed. Why not, when everything is possible? Anything.

My mother also instilled in me the belief that anything is possible, mainly that I could be and do anything I wanted, but Dickey's perspective was wider than my mother's. His mindset was always one of boundless possibilities, as in options. When my yellow lab, Dillon, whom Dickey knew—whom Dickey had seen leap like a stag, cavorting like the crazy dog he was—was injured, and bumbling medical care led to a situation wherein his leg was about to be amputated at the hip, I heartbrokenly told Dickey. He immediately exclaimed in horror, "Don't let 'em do it! There *must* be another way." And so there turned out to be.

A veterinary surgeon who had treated Dillon in the past finally agreed that if I would take him to the Columbia Boot and Brace Shop and have him outfitted with a prosthesis, he would amputate only the foot—for the time being. We went through prototype after prototype until the good folks at the prosthetic shop came up with one that would stay on the nub of Dillon's leg and actually work. The surgeon presented a paper on the procedure at an international veterinary conference and the protocol for that type of amputation completely changed. There were even news stories and a bit of fame for Dillon the wonder-dog and his canine prosthesis—all because Big Jim Dickey implored me to believe in possibilities beyond the predictable.

As I look back on it now, what I see in operation is Joseph Campbell's dictum to *follow your bliss*—the mantra by which I try to lead my life. *Follow your bliss*, Campbell says, *and doors will open where once there were walls.* It was Dickey, of course, who taught me about Joseph Campbell. Who taught me about so much—I, along with the hundreds and hundreds of others who stepped into that magical classroom where all was possible. The one where he lumbered up to the door with dozens of keys jangling from his belt and unlocked the portal to another realm.

Here is Pat Conroy recalling what Dickey told us: "Be afraid of nothing, he would say. Listen to what is real and essential inside yourself. Make yourself ready to embrace the spirit of the unknown and the unknowable. . . . Be open to all things, fully alive, the poet with arms out-stretched, ready for anything the world or God would fling your way . . . ." (Conroy xv).

Time and time again, long before he became deathly ill, Dickey would say to me, "Now, when I'm gone from here, you listen out for me on the celestial wireless." I have listened, and over the years I have heard, have felt his presence in both obvious and unexpected ways. When I open the pages of his work, they come alive with his voice. When I give public readings of his poetry (as I did, for example, at Pat Conroy's memorial service—Conroy, who referred to me as his Sister-in-Dickey) my voice is fueled with the fire of his power. When I teach my creative writing workshops every semester—in much the same way he conducted his own classes—his spirit abides. When I walk through the Horseshoe, I pace myself to accommodate his trundling gait and smile at the negative capability of him alongside me. This is expected.

Unexpected have been the moments of happy chance over the years when he has made his presence known in marvelous preternatural ways. The first time it happened, he came to me on the wings of a Monarch butterfly the weekend he died. (The inscription in the compact volume of Audubon's *Birds of America* he gave me that last Christmas reads, "Love from all the creatures of the air— including James Dickey.") We both hold a fascination with winged things, so it shouldn't have been a surprise to me that he sent—or showed up as—a Monarch.

The most recent happy chance was a few months ago, prompted

by the invitation from Bill Walsh to serve on the *James Dickey Review* advisory board. I was sitting on the dock at our (my husband's and my) fish camp on our little salt marsh island in the Carolina Lowcountry, thinking about Dickey, remembering some of what I have just shared with you. I'd been watching a pair of Bald Eagles much of the afternoon, and when I heard movement in the water, they were the first possibility that flew to mind. In the nanosecond it took for me to sit up and look to the source, I already knew an eagle would have created more of a crash if it had nailed a fish. I also knew that it wasn't the motion of a dolphin or otter—the other usual suspects.

When I saw that there were deer swimming across the river, my heart sang with pure delight. They had been stealthier than my ears could discern when they slipped into the water, but I watched the pair of them—incredibly strong swimmers that they are—make their way to the distant shore. Their underwater stride was swift enough to create small splashes across their broad backs and leave a wake in the tidal river behind them.

As they reached the other side, before continuing into the marsh and through the half mile or so of it before they could gain a foothold on dry land, the first thing they did was take stock—one looking left, one right—their pink-red ears aglow in the late afternoon sun. It was an amazement to witness them then slog into the pluff mud suck-of-shore where you or I would have sunk and been paralyzed in the muck—and on they trudged, invisible once they entered the thick sanctuary of spartina wetlands and once more became "unknown and unknowable."

You Dickey aficionados are put in mind of "The Starry Place Between the Antlers," I know—but it wasn't night and there were no antlers. That's okay—just a slight revision on Dickey's part. That he arranged for their glorious passage, I have no doubt. And as much as I reveled in their crossing, I couldn't help but wish they had swum from the other direction—toward the refuge of our island and away from the threat of mainland shotguns. But before they entered the secret marshland, the second Dickey-deer turned and looked me straight in the eye.

Do not despair, he signaled. *I will return. Listen out for me.*

In *Summer of Deliverance*, Chris Dickey writes, "Jim Dickey loved the power of coincidence, the way it defeated logic and created a sense of magical surprise in his life—in anyone's life. And he was even more intrigued by the power of dreams to defeat time. He liked to cite a line from the French poet Gérard de Nerval, who said the dream is a second life, and liked to believe that this second life was where the best poetry could come from. My father wanted to believe that in your dreams you could travel backward and forward in time, and the phenomenon of coincidence was somehow part of that" (175).

Perhaps such fluidity of time is what accounts for the experience that prompted me to write "Visitant." Perhaps time's cyclical nature somehow synchronized the past with the present for a long, long minute and allowed Dickey—not a dream of him in the usual sense (I've had those too) or the happy coincidence of a deer or butterfly— but *him* to manifest himself. Perhaps "dream" is the only label we know to assign the event because it didn't happen during hours of wakefulness.

In truth, explanation is irrelevant to me. What matters is that my friend Private Marion came to the kitchen window in the wake of a summer rain and touched his fingers to mine at the screen. What matters is the profound sense of comfort that remains, a reassurance that there is indeed more to existence than "the slings and arrows of outrageous fortune . . . the heart-ache and the thousand natural shocks that flesh is heir to." Mortality and what may or may not lie beyond the veil is a topic Dickey and I discussed at length, and he was always quite skeptical, so it's grand to know that Big Jim Dickey has not only discovered Hamlet's undiscovered country, but also that he found a way to elude—if only briefly—the place "from whose

bourn no traveler returns," to report back over the celestial wireless
that the unknown and unknowable are right there in the palm of my
hand, the one he kissed so long, but not goodbye.

Ellen Malphrus

Works Cited

Conroy, Pat. Foreword. *Classes on Modern Poets and the Art of Poetry*,
by James Dickey, edited by Donald J. Greiner. University of
South Carolina Press, 2004.

Dickey, Christopher. *Summer of Deliverance: A Memoir of Father and
Son*. Simon and Schuster, 1998.

Dickey, James. *Classes on Modern Poets and the Art of Poetry*, edited by
Donald J. Greiner. University of South Carolina Press, 2004.

James Dickey's Original Class Notes Transcribed: Hart Crane

This is the second installment of this enterprise, the first being published in the *James Dickey Review*, Volume 35, 2019. My introduction to that selection describes in detail the extent and nature of my Dickey class notes and what makes them of value to posterity. A large collection of Dickey's lecture notes was published in 2004 by the University of South Carolina Press under the title *Classes on Modern Poets and the Art of Poetry*, edited by Donald Greiner. Those notes represented a transcription of Dickey's lectures which were tape-recorded in 1971-72. My notes taken after those dates contain lectures on about twenty important poets not covered by the Greiner volume, along with notes on other important material. The following notes on Hart Crane were taken in Dickey's classes on February 11, 13, and 18, 1975. The lectures were delivered without prepared notes.

JAMES DICKEY LECTURES ON HART CRANE

Can a small-town candy manufacturer's son become a great mystical poet? (the soap opera approach) He can.

Born in Garrettsville, Ohio, Crane never even finished high school. The family lived in Chagrin Falls. Crane's Candies is still there. E.E. Cummings told JD [James Dickey] that Crane always claimed his father invented the hole in the Life Savers hard candy. [The claim is true.] Raised in Cleveland; his mother and father were classically incompatible. His father was a rather lusty type, his mother a rather fastidious woman—liked literature and art. She thought sex was vulgar (which it is—thank God). She didn't want a husband, she really wanted an escort. Hart was devoted to his mother. Homosexuality came of that.

What is ironic is that he was not destined to be a homosexual. He was very athletic, had a terrific build, was good at tennis. His type of homosexuality is interesting. He was a guy who loved other men, like Whitman. He liked tough, rugged guys, not effeminate ones. In New York, he hung out around seamen's bars, etc. A great number of them tried to take advantage of him, but he'd try to knock the shit out of them. Crane once told his friend the poet Allen Tate [1899-1979] that he "never could stand too much falsetto."

JD talked to the poet Yvor Winters [1900-1968, author of a major essay on Crane], who was supposed to meet Crane at the train station in Palo Alto. He said, "This can't be Hart Crane" on the platform. "He had the reticulated veins of an advanced alcoholic, white hair, cauliflower ears, bruised knuckles. I said, 'You're not Hart Crane, are you?'"

Crane lived like an engine with the governor off. A violent drunkard, he was an overt and aggressive homosexual. He liked to fight. He was afraid of no man, but he loved men. Some of his tenderest poems are to men. His mother was a singularly stupid and mean-spirited woman. His father was a pig-headed man who valued American commercialism. Hart always tried to get together with his father but never could. His mother wanted him to be educated, but his father not. Hart was horrified [by their marriage] and went to New York. The singular stupidity to turn a boy of 17 loose in New York City completely on his own resources is horrifying. But he shifted for himself, all the time working on poems.

He was entirely self-educated, out of three sources: 1) the bohemian intellectual life he fell in with in New York; 2) his own reading; 3) the literary magazines of his time. He devoured every issue of *Secession, Broom, The Little Review*, and others. He wanted to know where the action was, who the exciting writers were, who the good editors, etc. He taught himself French and German because he felt something terrific was going on there.

All the time he was working toward one goal: his own style. He was very single-willed. He knew exactly what he wanted to do. It was simply a question of how to get it. Everything he did was grist to the mill of his poetry—everything he saw, everyone he talked to. He had a devotion to the composition of poetry that few have ever approached.

He is a wonderful American and human sensibility. There are maybe sixty poems [in fact, just over a hundred]—a fastidious craftsman. JD has been to his cenotaph in Garrettsville, Ohio, and left flowers there.

He was also one of the most marvelous letter-writers ever—just as good as John Keats. He was so lonely that he just poured it out in his letters. They are very funny letters. He was an impossible guy to get along with, and someone you couldn't do without. He was blessed by having enormously sympathetic friends: Malcolm Cowley, Samuel Loveman his publisher, Allen Tate.

His mother's family had property on the Isle of Pines, a little island just off Cuba. He kept begging his mother to let him go down there. [JD tells a Jonathan Winters joke on learning a trade.] He appealed to philanthropist Otto Kahn, who gave him $1,000. So [mostly on the Isle of Pines] he wrote what was conceived of as an epic masterpiece, *The Bridge*.

It's commonly thought by critics that The Bridge is essentially a failure as a structural whole. It is not in any sense a concerted, depth-structured work. It consists of a number of related lyrics. His temperament was too volatile to develop a multi-structured long work. So it's a number of related lyrics, some of great power. But JD would take any section of *The Bridge* over anything in T.S. Eliot.

Back to New York, he's in the same old financial bind. He gets a Guggenheim Fellowship and cuts out again. He goes to Mexico, and sits down to read and research a poem on the conquest of Mexico. That poem had already been written by Archibald MacLeish [*Conquistador*, 1932]. But Crane wanted to do it in his own visionary style. But he's too far gone on alcohol. Katherine Anne Porter [1890-1980], his neighbor there, kept trying to help him. JD thinks by this time he was pretty close to insanity.

He tried to break away from his homosexuality. He took up with [Malcolm Cowley's estranged wife] Peggy Baird. But he was past the point of no return. The money ran out. In all the Guggenheim year, he only had a bunch of books with whiskey stains and one poem, "The Broken Tower"—one of the best he ever wrote.

[His father having died,] he thinks he can go back to save the family business. On a ship steaming out of Havana, he goes to Peggy's cabin and says he can go no further. She says, "You've just got a hangover." He jumps overboard, his last words "Good-bye, everybody."

Crane is one of those poets who, like Keats, was a great letter-writer. JD thinks Crane's letters are the best he's ever read. (Alexander Pope edited his own letters for posterity. Can you imagine that?) But Crane's letters are in an enchanting style, though unlike his poems. [JD reads one of Crane's homosexual letters written in Hollywood.]

He's such a likeable fellow. He wants to be a great American poet. He not only wrote about the problems of modern poets, he lived them. JD thinks he is really the central figure in modern American poetry. He was creatively intelligent. He had a very live mind.

1) He believed he had mystical intuition—insight into communal existence, the life of a people, of a civilization. JD mentions the letter where Crane describes the dentist's visit during which he experienced a mystical revelation of the future of America. His vision was not in any way religious; it was a *secular* vision. He refers to God only as the architect of the universe. He was fascinated by machinery. He felt the answer lay there—not like Eliot, who felt it lay in regression, the church, prayer, etc.

2) It was important to Crane to look on *The Bridge* as an answer to Eliot's regression and pessimism. Faith in technology: he was fascinated by the metaphysics of machinery. His is a very intense secularism. He believed in action, and in building factories.

The Brooklyn Bridge became his symbol by no accident at all. He thought it stood for everything he believed in. He felt it joined the old world to the new. He was always pointing to the open-endedness and infinite possibility of human existence. Like H.G. Wells, he believed man could build a new, better society, and also a new and better sensibility, more fellow-feeling, more sensitive.

He thought it would make people kinder to each other. Crane says, "One would think this environment would make men robots, but I don't. I think it would make them kinder, more gentle with each other." JD says in a cooperative enterprise like a mill or an army, you feel closer to people, but he's of a divided mind on the problem. Crane would have thought the Apollo space program to be his ultimate vindication.

3) His approach to language. He was a good and interested reader on linguistics, and how language operates. He bought a slide rule. He thought that kept him in time with the kind of man he wanted to see evolve. He evolved a theory of poetry that is uniquely his own. He came to think that the difference between the connotative and denotative value of a word—precisely that difference is what constitutes poetry. He was extremely word-sensitive. If JD says a light: burns, glows, radiates, shines, there's a difference in connotations. And Crane would say that connotation makes all the difference.

So he proposed to extend that to the logical end, but also to the *illogical* end. He conceived of poetry in which the impingement of words on the reader's mind would be the only thing that matters. [JD talks about Crane's famous 1926 letter to Harriet Monroe, publisher and editor of *Poetry* magazine, in which he explains and justifies his poetic method. Then JD focuses on the phrase "adagios of islands" in Crane's poem "Voyages II" (1924), which Crane discusses in his 1925 statement "General Aims and Theories." There Crane says ". . . the reference is to the motion of a boat through islands clustered thickly, the rhythm of the motion, etc. And it seems a much more direct and creative statement than any more logical employment of words. . . ."] JD says there's nobody now who doesn't steal from the Crane technique. He thinks Crane has had more influence than anybody.

Crane is a good prose writer. There are just a few reviews by him, especially the one on a photographer ["A Note on Minns" (1920)]. He was essentially a very deep critic. In his letters, he was a great explainer of his own works. There can be but very few people who have commented on their own work so much. [JD reads from Crane's short essay "Modern Poetry" (1930).]

You can't be neutral on Crane. You either do or don't think he's the greatest thing you ever saw, that he opened a new avenue for English poetry. A poet who lived a tragic life and died the death of a hero. JD says he once thought of writing an article to counteract

The Savage God (1971) by A. Alvarez, to be called "The Suicide Certification," the notion that suicide validates a writer's work. JD of course believes it doesn't.

JD reads about Crane from D.S. Savage, The Personal Principle: Studies in Modern Poetry (1944), a book that counteracts Eliot's autotelic art doctrine that a literary text is sufficient unto itself. Savage's book is very brave. He says the only thing that's important at all is the imprint of the personality on the poem. JD agrees. It's a fine antidote to Eliot's impersonal and machine-like approach to poetic creation. [JD here begins a sort of dialogue with Savage's book on Crane's work.]

Savage: The relationship of the poet to an industrial society—that determines the whole sensibility of a culture: it is the poet who can tell us this. It is a great theme that Crane took on. If it was too great for his powers, you could only say that it's too great for anybody's powers—just like Milton's case. He embraced his life and times feverishly with open arms. Like Mayakovsky he died of his own hand when his dream for his world was not to be realized. He possesses a largeness of theme—with delicacy and confident power of execution. His work is obscure, however. His collected work appears fragmentary.

Dickey: Crane should be read for his great lines. He had poor structural power. He wrote in an inimitable way that opens something to the human sensibility that we would not otherwise have. He is "among the English poets," like Keats hoped for himself.

Savage: Poetically, according to his own aims, he must be judged a failure. But what was he trying to do? A man of the cities, son of commercialism. Socially and regionally he was rootless. He was particularly vulnerable to the impersonal aspect of modern experience. In the end he became economically parasitic.

Dickey: It is because he was so completely at the mercy of his time that makes him so interesting. But with this there was an open acceptance of the achievements of American technological civilization, while detesting its commercial aspects. At the same time he felt the artist's alienation. It was on this cross that he allowed himself to be crucified.

Savage: Crane felt from the start that Eliot was the enemy, the one who wanted to take us away from the magnificent technological potentialities of a secular society, back into the Middle Ages. He admired Eliot's technique, but deplored his attitude. Eliot's *Waste Land* of rubble and desiccation vs. Crane's *Bridge* above and beyond disharmony and disintegration. Crane's ignorant, powerful mind went toward ecstasy, delight, affirmation.

Dickey: Crane's poem "For the Marriage of Faustus and Helen" [1923] is a chaos of incomprehensibility, but beautiful in its individual effects. For him, modern progress was a reality. He felt that we had the world, but didn't have the poetry that would spiritualize it. And that was what the poet is for—to make us come into harmony with that which we have made. This is a mighty theme, and sometimes he's a mighty poet. JD likes a guy who would try to do that, ignorant as he was. To go up against the whole literary establishment—to make an enormous reversal of human and cultural values by means of his poems.

Crane says we have made a world that has never before existed, but we don't feel the spirituality of our own achievement. And it is the poet's job to make us feel that. And if we can't do it, we deserve to be automatons. But Crane thought he could do it, and he was going to do it by writing his poems. He saw Eliot as somewhat cowardly, a little weak in the knees. Crane was enormously virile and active.

He loved the city like Whitman did—a place of enormous possibility—so much chance for encounter, so much human possibility. But to Eliot the city is unutterably revolting. To him it was a lot of human dreck, fruitless jobs, revolting physically. JD says he's had his time of feeling both ways. Eliot sees the city as a place where every man is alone, where most people are wretchedly unhappy. He sees it all as phantasmagoric, like a scene from *Limbo*. Not noble enough to be Hell either, it's Purgatory, the place where one waits with nothing to do, nothing to do. So Eliot will quote Dante in Purgatory. JD says the writing of Crane's friend Gorham Munson [1896-1969] is worth one's while.

Savage: To put positive and glowing spiritual content into

machinery was what Crane tried to do. (JD says Crane always kept a slide rule with him, to keep him in touch with his culture.) He wanted to give an inward spiritual significance to the outward mechanical manifestations of technical America. His effort was heroic and pathetic. We should be grateful that one poet undertook a task such as this, for the lesson he leaves for others, but also for charting an area that would otherwise be uncharted. Into his experience he tried to incorporate the whole of American urban society. [Reference to Savage's book ends here.]

[JD reads Katherine Anne Porter's account of being Crane's neighbor in Mexico, from Philip Horton's biography *Hart Crane: The Life of an American Poet* (1937).]

All the time he wrote, Crane was working consciously toward a style that would be identifiable as his. This is one of his first poems, not a Crane poem but a beautiful poem. [Reads "My Grandmother's Love Letters" (1919).] His nature was almost entirely developed from teen age with people who were interested in the arts. He used to spend a lot of time in the attic reading, hence the scene of this poem. The poem has its faults. "Through much of what she would not understand" is straight out of "J. Alfred Prufrock," but "It is all hung by an invisible white hair" is the vein that will become the great Crane style.

[Reads "Episode of Hands" (1920).] In "My Grandmother's Love Letters" and in this poem, you can come into contact with a vein of sentimentality that is not good. But this poem is good, with one magnificent image in the second stanza, of machinery, blood, and sunlight:

[The gash was bleeding, and a shaft of sun

That glittered in and out among the wheels,

Fell lightly, warmly, down into the wound.]

This poem does verge over into the abyss of sentimentality, conventional and romantic, but the sharp focus in the second stanza is not: that is specifically and very powerfully observed. JD wishes Crane had pursued that part of his talents more than he did—more about human relationships. He *began* with people and ended with great ecstatic visions of civilizations and so forth.

[Reads "Black Tambourine" (1921).] This is the transitional poem. We move into something much more symbolical. JD knows no poem that gets the implications better of the removal of the black man from Africa. This is the poem that raised a stir, written by one so young. Twelve short lines. A remarkable piece of work for a kid, so many implications there. JD quotes Matthew Arnold for comparison: "Wandering between two worlds, one dead, / The other powerless to be born." [from "Stanzas from the Grande Chartreuse," (1855)]. Arnold's good—you should go back and read him.

He moves at last into the Crane idiom. A poetry in which there is almost nothing to be understood and everything to be felt. [JD reads "Emblems of Conduct" (1923)]—one of his favorites. To do a denotative study of that, you could go on forever. (Tennessee Williams' play *Summer and Smoke* [1948] takes its title from this poem.) To read Crane, you don't have to torment yourself with exegesis. You have only to go back to the single line. "By that time summer and smoke were past." Now just get that relationship. It boggles the mind how good that is.

When you lecture on a poet, you want to get the essence of him. Who can do that? JD read Crane in foxholes in the war. He didn't move him but he excited him, interested him. Now, thirty years later, JD has come to a reconciliation of his ideas on Crane.

Crane's reputation: he was given a Guggenheim fellowship. The man responsible for administrating the fellowship, Henry Allen Moe, predicted that Crane's name would be high among those of the American poets of his generation. The essence of Crane we won't know, any more than Goethe says in reference to God (it requires a great arrogance to write about God): a choir of angels sings, "Thine aspect cheers the hosts of heaven, / Though what thine essence none can say"—from Louis MacNeice translation of *Faust* [1949]. Crane's life is endlessly fascinating. JD recommends the biographies, Philip Horton's [1937] and John Unterecker's *Voyager: A Life of Hart Crane* [1970], and Crane's *Letters, 1916-1932* [ed. Brom Weber, 1952].

Let's look at the structure of *The Bridge*. He was fascinated by the sea, ships, and travels. *The Bridge* is conceived as a major work. Crane thought big. It was going to be a big work, and it was going to take the American language into the equivalent of the great flowering of literature in Elizabethan England. He thought he could take his discoveries and turn the world around, so that it would never be turned back. We would go with hosannas into the factories, and see all that we have made as good. And the language would be different. It would change the whole sensibility, and the poetry of all the people who came after him.

Crane believed in the dynamism of language, in its ever-changing potential—fluid, always moving, always new concepts and new images. He ransacked newspapers, technical journals, medical journals, etc., for the things that would enable him to write the kind of poetry he wanted to write. What he wanted to do in *The Bridge* was to show some of these things and employ the language in this way. He went for the connotative use of language. Everything is an explosive metaphor which has to do with his own ecstatic apprehension of the future of America.

The Bridge is the symbol of past and future, old and new, the past and the machine age, consciousness and unconsciousness. It's a great tribute to his vision that he is able to convey these multi-level meanings and still keep a tremendous rhetorical drive going. He had a great range of effects. He can be gentle and strange, or rhetorical and infinitely strange. If you haven't read him, you couldn't believe it is possible to do what he did.

[JD reads "To Brooklyn Bridge," and comments on each stanza.] He is great with totally unexpected openings that can pull you right in. What other poet would have started with a rhetorical question that's not a question? The first line includes the great phrase "rippling rest." In the first stanza, he acts like a filmmaker to the Statue of Liberty. In the second stanza he's already gone to an office in the city, and the shadow of the seagull crosses a page of figures. The third stanza shifts to the cinema, people lined up as if to say, "Boy, have you seen *Deliverance*? You've got to see it." The movie is our version of the prophetic vision.

In the fourth stanza, the bridge is anchored in space and time, but still is eternally free. In the fifth stanza, the suicide is the bad part of modern life. In the sixth stanza, the line "A rip-tooth of the sky's acetylene" is one Robert Lowell thinks is the greatest line ever written. "Acetylene" is one of those technical words Crane seized upon. Stanzas nine and ten are the best. "The city's fiery parcels all undone" is the greatest line. Crane doesn't have to say it: he puts all his poetical chips on being able to imply it, and he damn near pulls it off. He is implying that we have created a new kind of heaven that God would do well to pay attention to and learn something from.

He wanted for *The Bridge* a kind of circular organization, and to wind up at the end on the bridge again, as he does with the final section "Atlantis." America would be the *found* Atlantis. He goes into an enormous musical figure: the notion of the bridge as a gigantic musical instrument, which reconciles all opposites (in the Platonic sense). The epigraph of the poem evokes a symbol of the melting-pot quality of America. In "Atlantis" he gets tremendously rhetorical at a high Miltonic pitch. A little bit shrill, but he never loses control. The sheer velocity of the thing, and the immediacy with which he throws one wild image after another is marvelous, *exhilarating.*

He has a cinematographic view of poetry. He gave his life for that kind of writing. He lived and died for it. There is some bad writing in *The Bridge,* too. He just tried to ram it on through, and the system fell flat on him. So, there are some terrible parts of *The Bridge.*

[JD reads Elizabeth Hardwick's review of Crane's *Letters* in her book *A View of My Own* (1962). Then he finishes by reading a paragraph from Allen Tate's essay about Crane.]

James Mann

The Handy Man

I was living in Northern California—my children grown—partnerless, and overdue to deliver a book, but every week another calamity interrupted my work. Things at my house kept breaking down and there was nobody to fix them. You could say I had a handyman problem. And a man problem in general.

In the fifteen years since my divorce, I'd had a number of relationships. I'd never been someone who placed status or money high on the list of what I sought in a partner. But at some point, I'd come to actively distrust those things. When you've had the experience, multiple times, of discovering that someone who looked good on paper turned out to be bad news in life, the corollary might apply: that someone who looked bad on paper might be just who you were looking for—a man with a big heart and a strong moral compass. He should passionately and unwaveringly adore me and be capable of inspiring my love in return. Good hair—a feature I never considered when younger, before the men in my age group started going bald—would be a plus.

I could earn my own living (though I needed badly to deliver that book). I wasn't skilled at home repairs, but I could always hire one of the Guatemalan men who stood outside Home Depot. It helped that I spoke Spanish—acquired from years of spending time at a house I owned in a village there. One good thing about my life as a solo operator was how free it left me to take off when I chose. There was nobody waiting for me back home. This was the good news and the bad.

At the moment in question, I'd turned the lower level of my California house into an apartment to help with my children's college tuitions. Mostly, this worked well, but my current tenants were a challenge. They had recently covered their windows with black cloth. They set out bowls of food for the raccoons, who now congregated on the deck. Sometimes I heard loud arguments below. Other times, crying.

After I tried to pay this couple a visit to discuss these issues, they set a pile of stones next to the door which, they informed me (speaking from behind the black fabric) they would feel justified in pelting in my direction if I approached again. My county's tenants' rights laws made eviction nearly impossible.

One day my tenants' stove stopped working. It turned out they had a thing about Sears repairmen. This was how I came to meet Peter.

I found him on Craigslist. "You won't believe it," he told me. "I'm at your exit. I'll make everything right as rain."

How do I describe the man who showed up on my doorstep twelve minutes later? Start with his old truck—no three pieces of side panel painted the same color, the hand-built roof rack piled high with treasures.

He stood couple of inches shorter than I and looked a good ten years older. He had the kindest face and the bluest eyes I'd seen outside of a Paul Newman movie and a full head of beautiful silver hair.

I'd just made coffee. That sure would hit the spot, he told me.

Something about Peter inspired me to tell him the full story of my difficult tenants. When I got to the part about the raccoon babies in my walls, he closed his eyes as if this latest information required even greater concentration. Then, toolbox in hand, he set down a set of outside steps—also in need of repair—to the apartment below.

Four hours had passed when Peter returned. "Everything's good with those two," he said.

How was this possible?

"I asked them to pray with me," he said.

Peter followed a guru whose teachings had guided him all his life. He and my tenants had sat together on the floor for an hour as Peter led a Buddhist chant. After, he'd fixed the stove.

"They've been going through rough times," he explained. "Lost a baby. We prayed over that too."

I had more jobs for Peter.

"I bake pie," I said. "Next time you come, there'll be a slice waiting for you."

What do you know? He had a bucket of fresh-picked blackberries on the front seat.

"I could take care of that railing on your deck," he said, when he returned with the berries. I took out my rolling pin. Before he took his first bite of pie, Peter bent his head, with that beautiful silver hair. He sat that way, saying nothing, for a surprisingly long time before lifting his fork but when he did his face seemed lit with pure joy.

That night we became lovers.

I have tried to reconstruct how we got from my kitchen table to my bedroom. I can't remember the sequence of events that got us there because events had nothing to do with it. With Peter, it was about a feeling I had that this was a good man with a rare and undefinable gift and the purest heart. He was like a wizard, an animal whisperer, a visitor from another galaxy. Within a day of that first visit, the tenants took down the black curtains. The racoons went away.

"I told them they had to find another home," he explained. Meaning the racoons, not the tenants.

Once and once only I visited the shipping container where he slept, on a thin cotton pallet with a framed picture of his guru beside it and a set of old golf clubs. He was a scratch golfer but seldom played. Greens fees were a problem.

He cooked for me—vegetarian dishes containing unidentifiable spices. He read me poems in Sanskrit, a language he did not speak. He told me if I ever needed a kidney (not that I did) one of his was available.

One time during this period, my children paid a visit, and we went out for sushi. Peter was quiet during the meal. I knew my sons and daughter would find him a surprising choice as a boyfriend, but they were open-minded people and wanted me to be happy. Before we parted, he spoke to the three of them.

"Your mother is a beautiful human being," he said. "Never forget this." They nodded, looking vaguely shell-shocked.

I loved Peter, but his fierce animal love occupied a whole other dimension. He had no money, but he never showed up at my house without a present—an earring he made from a feather. A bangle from India. He'd worked full-time since he was fourteen, raised five children, taught golf lessons, trained dogs, travelled to India. He was not what you'd call a raconteur, but his stories never ceased to amaze me.

The problem had to do with me. At the time I met Peter, my book deadline had been extended twice, and work was not going well. I'd sit at my laptop while he tinkered, but when I looked up, he'd be staring at me.

"I love watching you type," he said. "I love watching you think."

Then came new trouble. A landslide hit my house in Guatemala. The damage was huge. Reports from my village spoke of rivers of mud, and piles of rocks, fallen trees. Mess, everywhere. An idea came to me. I bought Peter a ticket to Guatemala. The plan: he'd stay at my house for six weeks and oversee the repair work. He could take Spanish lessons. If he learned some basics, when he came home he could hire a crew from among the hard-working Guatemalans outside Home Depot. They'd have an equitable boss with a truck and tools. Maybe he'd get on his feet financially. A good thing for everyone.

I drove Peter to the airport. "I'm going to get that place of yours ship shape," he said, when I kissed him goodbye. "When I come home, I'll *habla espanol* better than Speedy Gonzalez."

Amazingly, he made it to my village, on a chicken bus. Every night he called with updates on the repair work. About the Spanish classes, he spoke little.

"This old brain isn't what she used to be," he said.

Back home, my book was nearly complete—a huge relief. But a question loomed: What did I think was going to happen with Peter? Suppose he actually managed to get a crew together, find jobs, move out of the shipping container? What then?

Eight days into his time in Guatemala, Peter called me. "I hate to let you down, baby," he said. "I just miss you so much."

He was at the airport already. The flight was about to board.

I spotted Peter from his work boots as he descended the escalator at SFO. Then the rest of him came into view. Same kind face, lit up with a joy I had not witnessed—with me as its object—since my children were very young. One thing was different—his hair. It was black as the night.

He held me for a long time, so tightly it was hard to breathe. His head smelled of dye. "Why did you do this?" I asked him.

"I just wanted to look young for you, sweetheart," he told me. A terrible sadness came over me then. Here, finally, was a good man who would do anything to win my love. Too much.

In the car, I was quiet. "You're disappointed in me," he said. I offered no reply.

The next day, I told Peter I had to work all week. I had bought tickets to a concert. He could come for dinner, then we'd go hear the music.

"I never went to a concert before," he said.

The day of our date, Peter showed up at two o'clock, holding flowers. Also, a set of placemats and a magnet from the Guatemala City airport. He wrapped his arms around me in the way I always thought I wanted.

"I told you five o'clock," I said, hearing the coldness in my voice. *Hating it.* "I was working. You showed me no respect."

"I'll just sit quietly," he said. "I can fix that front step."

"*No.*"

He clutched harder. I turned my face away.

Then he was grabbing me. Then he was shaking me. "I love you so much," he said. Over and over, the words I had missed for so long.

Except for once when I was twenty, when a stranger pushed his way into my motel room and raped me, I had never been afraid that someone might physically injure me. That man didn't even know my name. This one was telling me he loved me more than anything on earth, as his large hands circled my neck. For a moment, the thought occurred to me that if he didn't release his grip I could die.

161

"Get out," I said. "I can't be with you anymore, ever again." I was not the only one weeping.

Then, like the raccoons, he was gone.

Peter stopped by my house one more time. He left a letter on my doorstep. He understood he couldn't be with me anymore. He had spent three days in prayer.

"I will always love you," he wrote. Title of my favorite Dolly Parton song. He left me a framed photograph of his guru. "If you are ever in trouble, call on him," Peter had written.

The strange, sad tenants moved out that summer. My book came out the following spring. I had learned, long before this, that anyone who ever supposes the publication of a book might serve as the gateway to a happy life has another thing coming.

Some years after I said goodbye to Peter, I met Jim, who drove an old Porsche Boxster, not a truck, but also possessed a kind heart, and a moral compass, and capacity to love me in a very large way, though never so much that I feared for my life. We got married and lived together until the day of his death from pancreatic cancer. The loss was brutal.

Five years have passed since then. Many more, since Peter showed up with his tools and his blackberries and his large, too-loving heart.

Two years ago, I decided to go online, no longer in search of a handyman but rather, a good partner. The tallest order. The man who loves me now—the man I love back—is happy when he sees me, and fine when he doesn't. He tells me he wants to spend his life with me. He also prefers watching Knicks games alone, same choice I make when tuning in to episodes of *This is Us*.

This man is not remotely handy. But certain things that matter most, he knows how to fix.

Joyce Maynard

The Act of Killing in James Dickey's *To the White Sea*

James Dickey's debut novel, *Deliverance*, placed readers alongside the struggle of four weekend warriors as they fought for survival, following a brutal attack in the backwoods of Georgia. For these characters, white collar suburbanites all, violence does not come as a natural impulse, even when the act of killing may stand as the only option to avoid death. Upon the book's publication in 1970 (and in the 1972 feature film), readers were startled by the implications of what seemingly ordinary men could do when pushed to their mental and physical limits and by the moral compromises involved with the act of killing. By dropping his readers in the middle of the harrowing situation of his characters, Dickey asked his audience to consider the implications of their actions as a means of survival.

What then, might an audience make of a man who existed outside of those moral restraints and felt at liberty to kill as his right? Dickey's third and final novel, *To the White Sea*, explored these issues through the character of Muldrow, an unrepentant World War II soldier who fights his way across Japan after his plane crash-lands in Tokyo. Unlike the protagonist, Ed Gentry from *Deliverance*, Muldrow finds it easy to leave behind a trail of corpses as he murders his way towards northern Japan. His instincts and moral character live far outside the realm of Ed Gentry, yet Gentry appears more corrupted by that novel's end. Muldrow has reached a state of near grace, despite his responsibility for a death toll akin to that of a serial killer. Taking such radical character stances borders on courageous or sheer lunacy for a writer like Dickey, but Muldrow exists outside of these moral barriers, and his killings mean something different than Gentry's. For Ed, murder becomes an act of desperation. For Muldrow, killing becomes an art, and the reader should interpret his actions as quests for purity and discipline instead of just the horrific nature of the acts.

Before addressing the issue of Muldrow's killing as a form of art, we must first consider why his killings constitute murder that differs from the kinds previously depicted in *Deliverance*. For Muldrow, a soldier trapped in enemy territory, he often kills unprovoked, but each

Japanese man and woman he encounters could potentially inform on him to their government's army, likely leading to his execution. Muldrow is crippled by the language barrier, noting, "Even if there had been one person in Japan friendly toward me, one who would do anything to help me, there was no way for me to find him. I didn't have any way to speak to anybody, even to tell him I would kill him if he didn't do what I said" (*To the White Sea* 68).

To help the reader better understand the reality of the situation and the danger that he faces if caught, Dickey includes a scene where Muldrow watches on as an American soldier gets beheaded by a group of Japanese soldiers. Officers had warned Muldrow and his platoon about this potential danger if captured by the enemy, but the startling reality of the situation helps establish for both our protagonist and the reader that the rules of the Geneva Convention don't exist in this territory and that his risk is substantial. Muldrow sees the American beheaded with two swings of a samurai sword and watches the several cruel kicks delivered to the severed head before taking off into the woods (*To the White Sea* 103–105).

Dickey previously tackled World War II Japanese beheadings in his poem "The Performance." In this piece, the speaker remembers Donald Armstrong, a fellow soldier stationed in the Philippine Islands who was ritualistically decapitated by Japanese captors before collapsing into a makeshift grave he was forced to dig himself. The speaker remembers the sight of Armstrong performing handstands only days before his death. He imagines him at the time of his execution, reenacting those same physical feats in an attempt to amuse his captors and avoid certain death (*The Whole Motion* 58).

"The Performance" illustrates the cruel fates for many World War II servicemen captured by the Japanese. Beheadings were common, as were other forms of sadistic abuse, perhaps best seen in the barbarism of the Bataan Death March. Not only do the deaths horrify Dickey, but so do the lengths to which a doomed man will degrade himself in his final moments to avoid the blow of the blade against the back of his neck. Suddenly in those moments, acts of joy and humanity become desperate and ultimately hopeless attempts to avoid the inevitable. For the author, the dehumanization serves as a cruel addition to death. When faced with death, is it necessary to rob oneself of their dignity as well?

That he witnesses the American's murder does not necessarily justify the actions of Muldrow, but they create a situation meant to help the reader understand the incredible danger he faces. This execution scene strikes a strange chord when compared to *Deliverance* in which the centerpiece of the novel includes a vicious rape against Bobby Trippe and the subsequent killing of his rapist. Despite the similar life-and-death danger at play in that novel, the four friends take a timeout to convene about how they should handle the situation with the dead body. With the four friends confronting the situation from varying angles (rape victim, assault victim, killer, and bystander), their perspectives taint the experiences of how the others might handle the situation if they'd encountered it on their own. Lewis Medlock argues with Drew Ballinger to explain what he would have done if their positions had been reversed at the time the incident occurred, but the fact that the incident has ended makes Drew's reimagining of the situation meaningless. As Ed argues, "What we should or shouldn't have done is beside the point. He's there, and we're here. We didn't start any of this. We didn't ask for it. But what happens now?" (*Deliverance* 106). By addressing the obvious morality issues involved, the men, even those like Lewis and Bobby who show no guilt in their actions, can't escape the lingering sense of how things might have gone differently. Muldrow, on the other hand, does not suffer from those same issues.

In addition to the obvious threat found in *To the White Sea*, Dickey makes a point to establish a rationale to Muldrow's behavior early on in the novel to make the reader side with his survival tactics for the upcoming invasion. Like Lewis in *Deliverance*, Muldrow is a survivalist. The difference between both men comes from the fact that Lewis has become obsessed with preparing for a destructive threat he speculates will happen. A man consumed by personal improvement, Lewis's survival instincts develop less out of necessity and fear and more from boredom. As described in the novel's narration, Lewis's "capricious and tenacious enthusiasm" supplement insecurities to distance himself from the elements of his life he finds unsatisfying

(*Deliverance* 9). Ed says, "But in [Lewis's] mind he was always leaving, always going somewhere, always doing something else," a quality that impresses Ed but further suggests an instability in his friend (9). Lewis puts himself in dangerous situations like the rafting trip for an adrenaline rush that, for many readers, would make him appear dangerous.

Muldrow's justifications for his extreme nature make more sense in the narrative of *To the White Sea*. Part of the reason that Lewis's behavior appears more suspect to the reader is that his pseudo-philosophical musings come filtered through Ed's narration. Ed admires Lewis but also sees Lewis's behavior as an offshoot of his boredom with suburban existence. Meanwhile, Dickey opens *To the White Sea* with bombastic narration from a colonel describing the firebombing about to commence on Tokyo. Dickey's speech from the colonel takes perverse delight in the massacre about to take place on the city:

> Fire…We're going to put [the Japanese] *in* it. That's saying, friends, we're going to put fire around him, *all* around him. We're going to put it over him and underneath him. We're going to bring it down on him and on *to* him. We're going to put it in his eyes and up his asshole, in his wife's twat, and in his baby's diaper. We're going to put it in his pockets where he can't get rid of it. White phosphorus, that'll hold on. We're going to put it in his dreams. Whatever heaven he's hoping for, we're fixing to make a hell out of it. Soon, good buddies. We just got the good word this morning. White phosphorus and napalm. That's our good stuff for the little yellow man and his folks. We're going to make him a present of it, in his main city. Bestow it. Give it away. With both hands. With three hundred airplanes. Tokyo is going to remember us. (*To the White Sea* 1–2)

By opening *To the White Sea* with a monologue filled with such bloodlust, Dickey helps to create mistrust between the reader and the military complex. That the colonel can feel at ease with the mass extinguishing of Japanese citizens makes Muldrow's attitudes towards combat appear more rational. During the speech,

Muldrow is surrounded by fellow soldiers who take pleasure in their commanding officer's enthusiasm. Dickey uses the extremism of this speech as a contrast to the "country surrealism" spoken by Muldrow in his narration. Muldrow's surrealist language is meant to lend the character a lyrical, poetic quality not found in the other major characters of the story. Muldrow's groping attempts to articulate the sublime aspects of nature and the way he sees the world around him provide the character with a more endearing demeanor than the hard-nosed men around him who seek to snuff out nature (Clabough 139).

The two new recruits in Muldrow's company also help to establish his character as focused and knowledgeable in the skills of survival that appear more realistic when compared to Lewis. The more boisterous and aggressive of the two, Arlen, confronts Muldrow to assert his masculinity and try to intimidate the novel's protagonist. In the only brief insight into Muldrow's instability, the other new recruit tells Arlen, "Don't fool with him. The other guys told us that just as soon as we got in. Don't fool with this one" (*To The White Sea* 6). That line of dialogue might tip us off to the fact Muldrow has more unsettling qualities than we might expect, but his cool, informative demeanor comes off as gracious and wise when compared to the gruff nastiness of Arlen.

Additionally, Muldrow shows sensitivity to the other new recruits' questions, and his advice offers the reader a chance to side with and trust him. He first offers suggestions about shaving etiquette for the recruits' comfort when wearing oxygen masks for extended periods of time. His aggression never builds, and he compliments his other crew members as reliable when in an air fight. By the time conversation shifts to the materials Muldrow tapes to his person, the character has established himself as someone the reader can trust because Dickey has taken the time to write him as the most intelligent, logically driven person in the story. The fact that the story's narrative maintains such a close first-person perspective maintains our belief that Muldrow has valuable knowledge. The reader never questions the details of his survival tactics. When he speaks at length about the practicality of a repurposed butter knife as a combat tool, we trust the accuracy of what he says while never raising the question as to how he would know what a butter knife would do to someone used at close range. Although he's established himself as a veteran hunter, Muldrow probably never killed an animal in that fashion.

Muldrow's patience and understanding with the second recruit may be the most important scene towards helping the reader identify with the protagonist. The impending firebomb is a hellish and frightening scenario, and the reader should identify with this new recruit and his fears about the combat mission. When he asks Muldrow to walk him through the procedure and asks pointed questions about all his supplies, the new recruit acts as a reader surrogate who needs to feel at ease with the situation and Muldrow's character. Muldrow acts neither boastful nor uncertain in his explanations, helping to create a level of trust between character and reader. For this reason, we can push aside our questions as to why he kills his first several victims, particularly those in the Tokyo firebombing. The chaos and uncertainty of the situation lends the reader a certain confidence that Muldrow commits acts that must happen for the sake of his survival. Only as the body count rises does the reader look back at the death toll and question the necessity for so many kills.

In his own life, James Dickey made a point to distance himself from the character of Muldrow, saying that he and this killer had no resemblance. The character of Muldrow bore no resemblance to anyone he had known, nor did Japan reflect the country as it was at that time. Dickey argues, "If Japan is not like I say it is, it ought to be" ("Japan the Way He'd Like It"). Yet Muldrow does appear to have a faithful dedication to his bizarre ethics and beliefs that fall in line with Dickey biographies that portray the author as a fiercely independent and polarizing figure. As much as he might try to distance himself from the morality and actions of Muldrow, Dickey's codes fit with this character.

When Dickey wrote *To the White Sea*, it became important for the author to reestablish himself as a viable figure in the literary community after many people had written him off in the quarter century since the publication of his first novel. In a collection of Dickey's letters, editor Gordon Van Ness cites several key critics and family members who saw the author's career state in the 1990s as dead. He references critic R.S. Gwynn who argued Dickey's career as having "effectively ended after the appearance of *Deliverance* and his acting debut in the film version" (Van Ness 438). For Gwynn, "the mere mention of his name summons up sniffy dismissals... If a poet does not publish any work of unquestioned merit in a whole quarter of a century, no amount of spin control can save his reputation from a downward spiral" (438).

Dickey's own son, Christopher, who chronicled his relationship with his father in the memoir *Summer of Deliverance*, leveled similarly harsh criticisms towards his father and his experiences as a writer and world-class teller of tall tales. The memoir brought forth some interesting revelations about Dickey, like the fact that he'd never served as a pilot in World War II but rather as a radar operator (Kirby). Christopher Dickey saw the success of *Deliverance* (both book and movie) as a detriment to his father's career, "It seemed to me then and for a long time afterward that forces of self-indulgence and self-destruction, which were always there in my father but held in check, were now cut loose. And worse" (Van Ness 438–39). Christopher Dickey, while recognizing the tremendous virtues of his father, also saw how the man's faults destroyed the possibilities of what he might have done had he been more disciplined.

While the myth of James Dickey's life began to get the best of him during his later years, so did his personal turmoil. After the death of his first wife in 1976, Dickey married one of his graduate students two months later, the twenty-five-year-old Deborah Dodson. The whirlwind marriage with a woman nearly thirty years his junior brought considerable strain into Dickey's life, something his friend, author Reynolds Price, called "tragic" in Dickey's obituary. Dodson suffered from a publicly scrutinized battle with drug addiction and frequent arrests. Rumors persisted that she was physically and verbally abusive towards Dickey during their marriage. The emotional toll that Dodson brought into Dickey's life became a great strain on his personal and professional life, driving his children from his first marriage away in the process (Van Ness 35–36).

By the early 1990s, when Dickey began writing *To the White Sea*, the elderly author found himself grappling with lawyers and courts as his wife struggled with her demons. Now approaching his seventies and experiencing failing health of his own, Dickey found himself out of control of his own life in a way he had never experienced before, all the while raising a young daughter from his second marriage. In a letter to his editor, Marc Jaffe at Houghton Mifflin, Dickey lamented his growing troubles amidst the writing of his third novel. He found his troubles "so disheartening, so endlessly complicated with legalities, with medical solutions that don't work, with lawyers, doctors, psychiatrists, policemen, judges, probation officers, and God knows who or what else, that to lay all this on you would be an extreme unkindness, so I won't" (Van Ness 445).

According to Christopher Dickey, his father thrived on madness and enjoyed surrounding himself around people who might have been in leave of their good senses. He said, "But James Dickey was a dilettante of madness. . . . It was something he imagined, an idea he played with, like his diabetes, or killing a deer. Before Deborah, my father didn't have much experience of the real thing. None of us did" (*Summer of Deliverance* 239). In this sense, James Dickey bore a resemblance to characters like Ed or Lewis in *Deliverance*. In the case of both men, they have their romantic notions about what it would mean to rough it in life, but once life forces them to face those actual challenges, the romantic notions wither away. For Dickey, too, the romantic idea of insanity vanished when he found himself attached to a mentally unstable woman whose mind he could not wrap his head around. This situation only worsened with the presence of his young daughter.

Christopher Dickey also found disturbing the implications of the murders depicted in *To the White Sea*'s manuscript, as well as Dickey's unproduced screenplay. In an earlier draft of the book, Muldrow comes across some Japanese children whom he entertains by showing them some games before strangling them. At the insistence of his editor, Dickey excised this section from the book. The scene of the games remains in the finished novel, but the audience doesn't know what becomes of the children. Dickey's screenplay makes pains to insinuate that Muldrow may have strangled the kids. When Christopher Dickey read an early draft, he noted:

The screenplay made this a brief, odd encounter. But my dad wanted to draw it out, as it was in the novel, for all the tension it could hold. He wanted Muldrow to weave a string ladder with his fingers and hold it up against the moon for the children to see, and move it so the moon climbed the diamond shaped rungs. Then he wanted Muldrow to take this circle of string and hang it around the neck of one of the little children, so that, as you saw the knot at the throat, you couldn't be sure if Muldrow would strangle the little boy or not.

As my father talked I saw the string as he had woven it for me one afternoon on the steps of his mother's house in Atlanta in the 1950s. Maybe I was three or four. Anyway, I was still small enough for him to coax a thrilled little-boy laugh out of me by tossing me in the air on a long, warm afternoon after a Sunday dinner with the family. But he'd gotten tired of the game and wanted to show me another, and he had brought out a circle of string from someplace. 'I'm going to cut off my head,' he said, wrapping the thread around his neck, then lacing it through his fingers. And I knew it was just a trick. But my heart still picked up speed. (*Summer of Deliverance* 24–25)

Considering the disarray of his life at this time, I argue that much of the appeal Dickey finds in the character of Muldrow comes from the fact that his protagonist exhibits many of the traits the author himself failed to exhibit in his own life at this point in time. Dickey said of Muldrow, "like the character of any author, there are certain parts of your own personality that comes to the fore and you just maybe kind of exaggerate those. As the German poet Goethe says, 'The strength of my own imagination as a poet and a novelist is the fact that I cannot imagine any crime of which I myself would not be capable'" (Lieberman 448). The question remains as to how much of Dickey exists in the character of Muldrow. Did he, in fact, envision himself as the killer in those acts of murder?

While we may not necessarily ascribe the murders committed by Muldrow to part of Dickey's personality, I believe that the intense discipline and control that Muldrow commands over his life reflects Dickey's desire to reaffirm a foothold on his own life. Like the unfamiliar Japanese terrain for Muldrow, the personal and professional woes of Dickey were unfamiliar territory and were troubling to the aging author. A lone wolf like Muldrow must have appealed to Dickey. Muldrow remains a source of information, but he does not need to depend on the people around him for his survival.

Muldrow quickly eliminates each person he encounters who could serve as a potential impediment to his survival. Muldrow only appears to find solace in other loners like himself, such as the old man on the farm, the bear hunters, or the monk—all people who have comfortably removed themselves from the norms of society. Muldrow also respects those people with personal discipline and ethics that match his own. The reason he laments having to kill the aged samurai is that he recognizes the old man's considerable skills in the art of stalking his prey. His respect for the old samurai's skills prompts him not to take his attacker's sword: "I wanted to remember how the old man looked when he was coming after me, like the sword was a part of him, and the air in front of him was like a net – not on fire exactly, but electric, sparking" (*To the White Sea* 178). Muldrow even takes splinters from the fallen samurai's bones to use as tools, acting like a hunter respecting his kill by utilizing different parts for many purposes.

In his notes on writing *To the White Sea*, Dickey lists Muldrow's resources as "his cool," "his purpose: to get to…the sea 'with ice in it,'" "concealment," and "his ruthlessness." The loner Muldrow even comes from Alaska, not yet a state at the time of the novel's setting, but a territory, symbolically placing him as an outsider among the other Americans in his service and at a distance from the American experience. Muldrow is shaped—both inside and out—by the environment that surrounds him… Even at this early stage, before we know much about him, Muldrow stresses the lonely autonomy of the habitat that forged him. It exists not "away from" specific places and objects, but rather "away from everything," a condition that reflects back upon the place itself… and the person who inhabits it: Muldrow (Clabough 130–31).

In addition to those characteristics that Dickey wrote into the character, the author drew on the notorious American serial killer

Ted Bundy as a source for inspiration. Bundy had a "conscienceless demeanor" and "enjoyed manipulating his appearance for the purpose of luring his victims to him" (Clabough 138). Although Bundy was a predator with ingenious strategies for manipulating his victims, both Muldrow and Bundy have little in common beyond that (138).

Sgt. Muldrow has qualities that make him stand out from the rest of his platoon, enough so that the new recruit mentions that they'd been warned about Cahill. Ted Bundy, on the other hand, did not exhibit these traits in the eyes of those people who knew him. His mother found him an ideal child. A politically active young man, Bundy served under several major Republican political campaigns and friends considered him a future candidate for senator or governor (Simon 23). Muldrow relies on intelligence and cunning to help him survive in Japan. Bundy, on the other hand, used qualities like his "physical attractiveness and civic virtue... as props for his premeditated crimes" (23). For Bundy, the need to manipulate the conventions of humanity became one of his greatest tools towards luring and eventually killing his victims. Bundy's best known trap for capturing his victims (all women) was to wear a sling around his arm and using this disability to create the illusion of helplessness. When the women dropped their guard, he could capture them for his perverse desires (23).

Muldrow lacks those qualities that Bundy had in attacking his victims. He relates more towards animals he has hunted in the past, disguising himself in the wilderness like a creature eluding its prey. He "imagines his actions in natural terms, shunning society based deceptions for the lethal instinctive cunning of rapacious beasts" (Clabough 138). According to Christopher Dickey, his father actually maintained a correspondence with Bundy from jail. While it's uncertain what they conversed about in their letters, these exchanges likely had an influence over *To the White Sea* (*Summer of Deliverance* 132).

For this reason, Muldrow's encounter with the bear-worshipping tribe becomes crucial to understanding his relationship with both human beings and animals. When these villagers rescue him and return him to health, Muldrow initially develops a trust in them because they have extended kindness to him. His existence as an American and an outsider causes them no concern. However, his first viewing of their bear den sets off an anger within him that he cannot shake:

> No matter how friendly they were, these were men like all the others, and they did the same things as the others. They waned bear meat and furs, and their guilt about it set up all that singing and dancing, and playing those twanging instruments that all sounded out of tune. I say screw that. The animals are a lot better, than the people. My heart turned around and locked. (*To the White Sea* 250)

When Muldrow has killed animals in the past, such as the swan, he has always done so as a means of survival. No part of the animal goes wasted. In these bear hunters, he sees something more horrific in their actions. The fact that he calls them "men like all the others" helps to show the divide he sees and feels with other people around him. Muldrow does not see himself as existing in the same moral universe. The ritual that the hunters build around their killings also insults him because he finds it insulting to be brought into their celebration as if it were an honor to experience it. While he respects the cleanness of the kill, Muldrow remarks, "I have seen bad things happen in my life, but never anything that made me as sick or as mean as that. I didn't care what I did to any of them" (*To the White Sea* 254). Considering the violence he has perpetrated on people over the novel, this lofty statement speaks further to his dissociation from other people. The hunt, in the way that Muldrow kills people, has honor. The other killings, he sees as forms of torture and disrespectful.

Laurence Lieberman says that, for Muldrow, the tribe has made war against his closest kin and feels betrayed more so because he initially felt intense affection for these people (please note that his reaction to being turned over to the Japanese army by the monks did not provoke a reaction nearly as strong). His experiences with the hunters were, in a way, Muldrow's last ditch efforts to reestablish himself as a member of society. The abuse he took beforehand at the hands of the soldiers could be accepted in their way because they fell under the act of war. When he kills the man who rescued him and flees to live on his own, this marks Muldrow's last transition from man to animal (Liebman 177).

To the White Sea does not offer the first instance of Dickey writing about this distinction between the killing of animals/humans and necessary/unnecessary killing. In *Deliverance*, Dickey shows Ed struggling with the same dilemmas found in killing without reason. As a skilled bowhunter, Ed goes out on the second day of their camping trip and spots a deer walking through the woods. When he takes aim with his bow, a clean shot to the animal's heart in range, he fails to hit his target. The survival of the group does not depend on Ed killing the deer, making him uneasy about the situation.

In his essay on *Deliverance*, Henry Lindborg discusses the way that all the men in the canoeing group have decided to play the roles of experienced woodsmen on their trip. Ed muses, "I liked the idea and the image, I must say. I touched the knife hilt at my side and remembered that all men were once boys, and that boys are always looking for ways to become men" (Lindborg 87). In Ed's mind, their canoeing trip offers the chance to fulfill a rite of passage, "but behind this merging of fantasy and fact, there remains a continuing sense of the dream, of unreality, of play-acting. 'There was something to act out,' says Ed when he knows the problem of the killer must be confronted. 'We were all acting it out,' he repeated later" (87). For Ed, so much of his experience with nature comes with references to "Indians on calendars" or Lewis as "Johnny Weissmuller in the old Tarzan movies" that treating the experience as reality becomes impossible until faced with the life or death decisions that follow (87). When confronted with the chance to kill the man on the bluff, Ed overcomes his hesitation, stating, "I was afraid that my concentration had blown apart under the recognition that he knew where I was, and some of it had, but not all. The shot had been lined up correctly; if the left arm had held he was hit" (*Deliverance* 163).

After Muldrow compares himself to a lynx or a rabbit at various points in the book, Dickey ends the novel by writing about how Muldrow tries to take his most elaborate step towards masking himself as an animal. Confronted with a squad of soldiers outside a shack he's escaped to, he empties his sack of swan feathers and rolls around in them before stepping out to face the armed men. He describes his last actions as such:

> I walked out and I knew I had found it, what I had been looking for all my life, in all the blood and the fucking and the right arm and the fast move, in everything I had done and everybody I had had to deal with. I knew I had found it, but up till now I had never had the full thing. In the wind the swan feathers fluttered on me, and I could have flown. I could have flown with the hawks and the swans if I had wanted to. But I didn't want to. I wanted to stand there. (*To the White Sea* 274)

Muldrow never states what the "full thing" he refers to is, but his actions would suggest that he means to make his final transition into an animal, with which he has more of a connection than any of the human beings around him. This action brings up a few interesting questions as to what he has attempted to achieve his whole life and how this might relate back to a serial killer like Ted Bundy. Does Muldrow consider himself an animal and not just animalistic in nature? By acting as he has in his methods of killing and his sympathies towards other creatures, can we assume he blends in more among animals than humans? As stated, Bundy worked hard to master the art of blending in among average people during his years as a serial killer. In the last interview conducted before his execution, he talked at length about how he felt he came from a good home with a loving family. He talked about all of the kind things he used to do for other people and girlfriends. He suggested the importance of behaving like an average, hardworking American while committing heinous murders in his spare time (Triplexchurch).

By the novel's conclusion, Muldrow has "Arrived at the inhuman sensibility necessary for his transformation," noting "all the time I'd been in Japan, all the time I'd been living, this seemed to be the truth of the thing: you can get to the perfect blend if you know exactly how to do it, and if the time is right." In the potential film version, Dickey had even imagined Muldrow "disappearing amid a heavy gust of snow while the Japanese posse fires at him" (Clabough 160). Reviewing all of these connections into Dickey's life, it is important to question how much he ended up empathizing with Muldrow by the final scene. Did he, too, wish to go off like a bird? His escape from the harsh realities of life would prove impossible, but in the character of Muldrow, he found the possibility for another existence.

Charlie Riccardelli

WORKS CITED

Clabough, Casey. *Elements: The Novels of James Dickey.* Mercer University Press, 2002.

Dickey, Christopher. *Summer of Deliverance: A Memoir of Father and Son.* New York, Simon & Schuster, 1998.

Dickey, James. *Deliverance.* Boston: Houghton Mifflin, 1970.

---. *To the White Sea.* Boston: Houghton Mifflin, 1993.

---. *The Whole Motion: Collected Poems 1945-92.* Wesleyan University Press, 1994.

"Japan the Way He'd Like It". *Newsweek* 30 August 1993, Vol. 122.9. *Academic Search Complete.* Web 3 May 2014.

Kirby, David. "Liar and Son." *The New York Times* 30 August 1993.

Lieberman, Laurence. "Warrior Visionary, Natural Philosopher: James Dickey's *To the White Sea." The Southern Review*, Winter 1997. Proquest Research Library. 3 May 2014.

Lindborg, Henry. "James Dickey's 'Deliverance': The Ritual of Art." *The Southern Literary Journal,* Vol. 6.2 (1974): p. 83-90. Jstor. 3 May 2014.

Simon, Robert I. "Serial Killers, Evil, and Us." *National Forum 80.4* (2000): 23. *Academic Search Complete.* Web 4 May 2014.

Triplexchurch. "Ted Bundy's Last Interview." Online Video Clip. *Youtube.* Youtube, 28 May 2008. 4 May 2014.

Van Ness, Gordon. "Ground Control." *The One Voice of James Dickey: His Letters and Life, 1970-1997.* University of Missouri Press, 2005.

BOOK REVIEWS

Shaping the Beautiful Accidents: Memory as a Metaphor for Survival in Joel Peckham's *Bone Music*

Joel Peckham. *Bone Music*. Nacogdoches, Texas: Stephen F. Austin State University Press, 2021. 90 p. $18 paperback.

On a February morning in 2004, while on a Fulbright scholarship in Jordan, Joel Peckham, his wife Susan Atefat Peckham, and their sons Cyrus and Darius were involved in a horrific car crash that took the lives of Susan and the oldest son, Cyrus. Peckham and Darius survived. Peckham had extensive nerve damage and underwent a lengthy operation to reconstruct his hip, but as he explained in a 2004 interview with Derek B. Miller in *The Interview Spot*, those scars do not tell the full extent of the accident: "I was also overwhelmed with grief and guilt." He blamed himself not only for the accident, but also for the unhappiness and resentment in his marriage. In recently published essays, a memoir, and especially in his poetry, Peckham has been trying to shape those awful circumstances and feelings of guilt in an attempt to make sense of the past and as a way of moving forward. Writing, for him, has become "an act of self-preservation" (Miller).

Peckham, Assistant Professor of Regional Literature and Creative Writing at Marshall University in Huntington, West Virginia, lives with his son Darius Atefat-Peckham and second wife Rachel, who also teaches at Marshall. A graduate of Middlebury College, he holds an MA from Baylor University and a PhD from the University of Nebraska—Lincoln. His nine collections include seven collections of poetry; a memoir, *Resisting Elegy: On Grief and Recovery* (2012); a book of essays, *Body Memory* (2016); and a scholarly monograph on Faulkner. His first full-length collection of poetry, *Nightwalking*, was published in 2001. He has appeared in several anthologies and is co-editor of *Wild Gods: The Ecstatic in American Poetry and Prose* (2021). His work has also appeared in *The Southern Review, American*

Literature, Prairie Schooner, The Mississippi Quarterly, and *North American Review,* among many others.

Bone Music, like much of Peckham's poetry, is autobiography turned into art. In these poems—really, imagistic prose paintings—the speaker takes the trauma of unexpected death and turns it into narratives of vivid imagery that focus on creating a living map for survival. The poem that best exemplifies how Peckham mines the depth of the accident and the aftermath of his recovery is the volume's title poem, whose origin resonates with two of the author's main themes: healing and music. In the Soviet Union during the 1950s and 1960s, X-ray films taken from hospitals and clinics were used to make improvised gramophone recordings of banned music. Called "ribs," "bones," or "bone music," the recordings were of low quality, but they were also cheap and could be played 5-10 times each. X-rays were cut into 7-inch discs and grooves were cut into them by special machines. These records were sold on the black market, and banned émigré musicians and "decadent" Western music finally could be heard.

In the title poem, Peckham gives a brief history of these "ribs" then shows the personal connection between bones being broken then healed and a life being made whole again: "I lay in a hospital looking at the x-rays / of my shattered hip... / which seemed to be whispering to me somehow, of choices, and / accidents" ("Bone Music" 73-74). The music he hears and the healing of the body come together, and the "fiery brightness" (73) of the pins and screws holding him together sends him a message of hope. As he dealt with "the problem of memory" (Miller), as he calls it, Peckham was more and more determined to be honest with his readers, thereby letting out the anger and resentment, but also showing gratitude that he and his son survived.

What distinguishes Peckham's poetry is its expansive style, perfectly suited to the theme of reflection and looking forward. Its unrhymed and flowing lines are held together as if the speaker were thinking out loud. The ebb and flow of its prosaic quality suggests a contemplative reflection that seeks wholeness but also admits to a darker side: "With his own idea of what the pattern / wasn't, with the joy and terror of building and / breaking" ("Prologue" 9). Many of the poems, such as "To the Woman I Backed Into at the Kroger Parking Lot," suggest someone speeding ahead, trying to look forward while also gazing into the rear-view mirror: "I'm still looking backward trying to see what / I missed and what I didn't, my own eyes in the mirror, looking for yours" (31).

The overall effect works well for Peckham because his vision is doubled and contradictory, perhaps owing to or heightened by the accident that cost him so much: "Somehow / holding themselves together by being far away" ("The Wreckage That We Travel In"). There is a powerful disjunction of past and present, as if the sudden shock of the encounter caused him to be an observer of both life and death as seen in "Any Moonwalker Can Tell You II": "To stand inside outside / on the highest hillside with all our faith and fragility" (38).

Another key element in these poems is the father-son connection that has been shattered in half. There is still one living son, which forces the speaker to examine the *why* of life and to work through the anger, suffering, and lost opportunities of his other son and the mother of both boys. In "Going Sideways," the speaker is trying to make sense of the image of his oldest son who "flew through a / windshield, shattering into memory" (41). Life has "a way of slipping / past our defenses" (41), and the speaker is caught between forming connections and having those connections forever torn away:

> And I will spend the rest of my life asleep while
> waking, listening while not listening, trying to escape from where
> I am and where I've been and will keep going (because I don't
> know how to stop) wishing somewhere back there somehow it
> could have all gone
> sideways (43).

Having irreparably lost that connection with his son, the speaker is haunted by it but determined to go on until memory is "broken into wholeness" ("Arrhythmia" 50). Existence is a wake-and-sleep searching and both a denial of and an embracing of that moment his son came through the glass: "I did not hear and can't stop / hearing. I did not see and can't stop seeing" ("Arrhythmia" 52). The wreck has clearly affected all of his senses, causing him to doubt what he knows and who he is. Only in his dreams can another outcome happen, but then wakefulness returns: "the gentle sadness and surprise that we are still here" ("The Locomotive of the Lord" 75). In a surprising way, loss gives the speaker a new appreciation for living: "Thankful / for the son you've lost in a shower of sparks and the son waiting for you / at the farm and how sometimes you find one in the other" ("The Locomotive of the Lord" 85). By trying to hear "the voice of the son I lost" (83), the realization of that death shakes the speaker's memory but shows him possibilities for understanding and growth: "This life is a beautiful / accident made of accidents we try to shape" (83).

Bone Music is a poetic guidebook to grief. If the living are to come to terms with great loss, we must internalize those moments of *what if* and allow ourselves to realize that "loss can be a deepening too" ("The Locomotive of the Lord" 80). As Peckham says in his 2014 interview, "good writing should be imbued with sentiment... It should engage us in struggle" (Miller). Dealing with the death of his wife and oldest son could easily have been too sentimental, too much a wearing-your-heart-on-your-sleeve crying out. For Peckham, an accomplished poet and writer, the struggle itself is just as important as the sentiment, as he painfully accepts his role in the guilt and anger. The collection closes on a hopeful message, however. The last poem, "The Locomotive of the Lord," is a nine-part summary of what the speaker has learned from grappling with the trauma. The metaphor of a speeding locomotive is very apt here, and the epigram from Jack Gilbert is telling indeed: "If the locomotive of the Lord runs us down / we should give thanks that the end had magnitude" (75).

Peckham notes, in that same poem, that we are "desperate for contact" (79), desperate to connect with one another, and "it is a privilege / to be restless and dream of throwing a perfectly good life away" (81). Through all he and his son have endured, there is still a magnitude to that destruction. Peckham sees the cosmos at work. The vibrations of his personal story reverberate to the stars and down to us, and we are more alive than ever, more aware, and more able to show gratitude: "Thankful for the / impact and the magnitude / even as you hurtle toward your destination, knowing that you must / get off this train. Knowing you will / be run down and through / again" (86).

Gary Kerley

The Rise and Fall of Man in Southwestern Virginia

Edison Jennings. *Intentional Fallacies.* Broadstone Books, 2021.
72 p. $16.50.

Why is it that we seem predestined to live our lives clinging to false doctrine designed to keep us mindlessly avoiding truth, in spite of daily proof that our misconceptions are irrational? In a time when having the loudest megaphone trumps reason, is there a place for critical thinking? Is there still room for true empathy? In his first full-length collection of poems, *Intentional Fallacies*, Edison Jennings explores the themes of falling from grace and its consequences, life and death, and what ultimately defines the sacred and profane. But perhaps most importantly, Jennings engages the reader to reexamine what they have been told to think, and instead, to use compassion as the way to find truth and understanding.

As in his previously published chapbooks (*Reckoning, Small Measures*, and *A Letter to Greta*), Jennings proves to be a brilliant observer of the people and places in his native southwestern corner of Virginia. While illuminating the defilement and subsequent ruin of the once beautiful—now dying—towns of Appalachia, he wastes no time with subtleties. Instead, he slices with precision, revealing a misunderstood and complex world.

Jennings searches for, and typically finds, dignity in the citizens of these dust-choked mining towns. Many of whom are simultaneously addicted to both substance and survival. In the poem "Country Song," a couple does what it takes to subsist in rural America:

and he drives a long-haul truck,
popping Addies to stay awake,
selling weed for an extra buck

to pay off their subprime loan
and not have their house repo'd.
"We're screwed," he says, "screwed to the bone."

And despite their flaws, or perhaps because of them, Jennings finds beauty and treats his characters with respect:

And though they get high, they somehow survive
and manage to raise three kids
(who say they'll visit, but never arrive).

Last night she held him while he was asleep
and heard him mutter, "ain't nothing will keep."
Whoever dies first, the other will weep.

Biblical references abound in many of the poems, juxtaposing the holy and the irreverent, a contrast no doubt common in many parts of the world but conspicuously predominant in the ancient hills of the eastern U.S. where Saturday nights and Sunday mornings can often be as different as, well, night and day. For example, in "Spontaneous Combustion," sheep farmers come up on a burning stump. One of the men insist it is a burning bush, where he then "... knelt and asked its name...." The two farmers begin drinking from a flask and joke about the divine imagery as they continue "working the meadows, drinking whiskey, mending fence, / sipping fire that maketh glad the heart of man."

Hinting at the Eden-like splendor that once existed in these rural communities, Jennings pulls back the curtain exposing the horror brought on by greed, poverty, loss, and hate. Through many of his poems in this collection, Jennings examines people who have been put in the ironic situation where, in order to live, they must dedicate their lives completely to the one thing that will ultimately lead to their deaths. In "Tipple Town," the residents desperately cling to religion and community as a major coal plant shuts down, eliminating jobs and leaving the town in a state of apocalyptic dystopia:

The coal dust settles everywhere,
and fish are dying in the creek.
Mama thinks death's in the air.
The coal dust settles everywhere.

Now Daddy drinks and doesn't care
that mining made his lungs real weak.
The coal dust settles everywhere,
and fish are dying in the creek.

Jennings lays bare the hypocrisy of having compassion for only those who look like us, believe in our own traditions, or come from our own towns. Three narrative poems, "Cold Spring Morning and the Grade School," "The Klansman," and "My Fascist" cunningly reveal how unconditional love can shelter appalling horrors in our families, friendships, and communities. How we unquestioningly allow love and hate to somehow justifiably coexist.

Jennings reserves his most scathing treatment to those who willfully refuse to acknowledge the plight of their community, those who succumb to the allure of greed, those who strive to prove their worth by denigrating their very own neighbors, those who use tradition to justify hate. Similar to the paradox of how destructive industries or substance abuse can be both sustenance and death to the poor, Jennings demonstrates how the self-proclaimed righteous deliberately excuse, or in many cases, embrace those in power who are often responsible for bringing them ruin. In "The Financier's Lenten Confession, A Dramatic Monologue," a rich man reveals that as long as he appears pious to the working class, he will continue to be revered despite his greed and manipulation.

And while these concepts certainly pertain to our current tumultuous times, they are not new observations. Far from it. They are simply extensions of time-tested manipulations observed in societies since the beginning of time. The cover Jennings chose for this collection (*Satan Watching the Endearments of Adam and Eve* – one of the many illustrations created by poet and artist William Blake for an 1808 edition of John Milton's *Paradise Lost*) is evocative and gives a hint of what is found inside.

To take the metaphor one step further, Jennings demonstrates our gullibility before or during our seemingly inevitable fall from grace.

The Dickey-esque poem "Rainstorm" tells of the youthful naivety of a reckless, hell-bound road trip "across the rich and sinful South." Jennings then explores the unspeakable grief that often accompanies our collapse such as in "Blue Plate Special," where a girl's father and her boyfriend share a dinner together after her untimely death.

The poems collected in *Intentional Fallacies* are not only the continuation of the story of the fall of man, but how we struggle with the consequences of decisions—those made by us, and those made for us. Jennings uses gut-punch imagery to paint a desperate landscape populated by soulful people struggling against dire situations, and yet still searching for love and peace and meaning. These poems are expertly crafted and easily accessible, especially those written in narrative free verse. However, it is perhaps the more structured poems, with their almost singsong rhythms and clever rhymes that are most memorable in the collection, evoking the oral tradition of storytelling that has been handed down across time, civilizations, and traditions in this small corner of the world and beyond.

Jon Sokol

CONTRIBUTORS

CONTRIBUTORS

Ward Briggs attended Washington & Lee University, where he first met James Dickey in 1963. After receiving his doctorate in classics from the University of North Carolina, he joined the faculty at the University of South Carolina, where he eventually became Carolina Distinguished Professor of Classics and Louise Fry Scudder Professor of the Humanities. He and Dickey were colleagues and friends for over 35 years. Briggs is the editor of *The Complete Poems of James Dickey* (Columbia, SC: University of South Carolina Press, 2013).

Annemarie Ní Churreáin is a poet from the Donegal Gaeltacht. Her publications include *Bloodroot* (Doire Press, 2017) and *Town* (The Salvage Press, 2018). She is a recipient of The Next Generation Artist Award from the Irish Arts Council and a co-recipient of The Markievicz Award. She is a former literary fellow of the Akademie Schloss Solitude in Germany and the Jack Kerouac House of Orlando. Ní Churreáin was the 2019-20 Writer-in-Residence at Maynooth University of Ireland and a 2020 Artist in Residence at The Centre Culturel Irlandais in Paris. Her second full-length poetry collection, *The Poison Glen*, is forthcoming with The Gallery Press in 2021.

Stephen Corey's *Startled at the Big Sound: Essays Personal, Literary, and Cultural* (Mercer University Press, 2017) followed ten poetry collections, among them *There Is No Finished World* (White Pine Press, 2003), *All These Lands You Call One Country* (University of Missouri Press, 1992), and *The Last Magician* (winner of the Water Mark Press First Book Award, 1983). White Pine will publish his new-and-selected poems, *As My Age Then Was, So I Understood Them* (which will include the poems in this issue) in the spring of 2022. In 2019, he retired after 36 years of editorial work with *The Georgia Review*.

Kim Dower was born and raised in New York City. She earned a BFA from Emerson College, where she has also taught creative writing. She is the author of four collections of poetry: *Air Kissing on Mars, Slice of Moon, Last Train to the Missing Planet,* and *Sunbathing on Tyrone Power's Grave,* which won the IPPY Award for best poetry book of 2019. Dower's poems have been featured on Garrison Keillor's "The Writer's Almanac" and Ted Kooser's "American Life in Poetry," as well as in many journals, magazines, and anthologies. She was city poet laureate of West Hollywood, where she lives, from 2016 – 2018 and teaches poetry workshops for Antioch University, UCLA Extension, the West Hollywood Library, and the Hollywood LGBT Senior Center.

Stephen Dunn is the author of *The Not Yet Fallen World, New and Selected Poems,* forthcoming from W.W. Norton in 2022. His awards include the Pulitzer Prize for Poetry, the Academy Award for Literature, the James Wright Prize, and fellowships from the National Endowment for the Arts and the New Jersey State Council on the Arts. Stephen Dunn passed away in June 2021.

Graham Foust teaches in the undergraduate and graduate programs in the Department of English and Literary Arts at the University of Denver. He is the author of several books of poems, the most recent of which is *Embarrassments* (Flood Editions 2021). With Samuel Frederick, he translated the final three books by the late German poet Ernst Meister, including *Wallless* Space (Wave Books 2014), a finalist for a National Translation Award.

Gary Gildner has received the National Magazine Award for Fiction, Pushcarts in fiction and nonfiction, and the Iowa Poetry Prize for his collection *The Bunker in the Parsley Fields.* His memoir, *The Warsaw Sparks,* is about the 14 months he lived in Communist Poland teaching American Lit at the University of Warsaw (a Fulbright prof) and coaching the city's baseball team. *My Grandfather's Book* followed a memoir about his Polish immigrant side and was a ForeWord Book of the Year. *The Capital of Kansas City* (2016) is his fifth and most recent collection of stories. *How I Married Michele*, personal essays, appeared in 2021. The two poems in this issue are from *Calling from the Scaffold*, his ninth collection of poems, due in 2022 from the University of Pittsburgh Press. He has read his poems at the 92nd St. Y, Manhattan Theatre Club, Shakespeare & Company in Paris, on NPR, and on the ferry crossing Lake Michigan. At 16, pitching his first American Legion game, he threw a no-hitter.

Timothy Green has worked as editor of *Rattle* since 2004. He's the author of the book, *American Fractal*, and lives near Los Angeles with his wife Megan and their two children.

Janice N. Harrington is the author of *Primitive: The Art and Life of Horace H. Pippin* (BOA Editions). She is also the author of *Even the Hollow My Body Made Is Gone, The Hands of Strangers*, and several award-winning children's books. She teaches creative writing at the University of Illinois at Urbana-Champaign.

Joanna Hill spent her professional career in publishing—first in production/design at The University of North Carolina Press, University of Texas Press, Louisiana State University Press, and later in marketing and management at the Swedenborg Foundation and Templeton Press. She is the author or co-author of four books: *The Power of Prayer around the World, Tiffany's Swedenborgian Angels: Stained Glass Windows Representing the Seven Churches from the Book of Revelation, Spiritual Law: The Essence of Swedenborg's Divine Providence*, and *Words of Gratitude for Mind, Body, and Soul*. Born in Chattanooga, Tennessee, and raised in Charlotte, North Carolina, she now lives in Idyllwild, California, in a cabin in the mountains.

Kincaid Jenkins was born and raised in the South and has traveled the world at large. His love of poetry began with a high school lesson devoted to the then recently deceased James Dickey. He has won numerous local writing and art contests. *The James Dickey Review* is his first major publication.

Gary Kerley, retired and living in Bermuda Run, NC, received his PhD from the University of South Carolina in 1980, where he audited Dickey's Seminar in Verse Composition. He interviewed Dickey and has written numerous reviews and articles on his poetry and novels. Most recently, he wrote about the personal and professional relationship between Dickey and Pat Conroy for last year's *James Dickey Review*. Kerley is a regular book reviewer for *Publishers Weekly* and has a review of Marlin Barton's "Children of Dust" in the fall 2021 issue of *The South Carolina Review*. In addition, three new articles he has written on Alice Friman, Paul Hemphill, and William Walsh will appear in the newly-revised online "New Georgia Encyclopedia."

Daniel Lassell is the author of *Spit* (2021), winner of the 2020 Wheelbarrow Books Emerging Poetry Prize, as well as a chapbook, *Ad Spot* (2021). His poems have appeared in the *Colorado Review, Southern Humanities Review, River Styx, Birmingham Poetry Review,* and *Prairie Schooner*. He grew up in Kentucky and lives in New York with his wife and children.

Michael Lucker is a writer, director, and producer with twenty years of experience creating film, television, animation, and digital media. After graduation from Boston University, he landed in Los Angeles where he worked for ABC, NBC, CBS and HBO before taking a job as assistant to Steven Spielberg at Amblin Entertainment on the feature films *Indiana Jones & the Last Crusade, Arachnophobia, Joe vs. The Volcano, Always, Back To The Future II & III,* and *Jurassic Park*. He has also worked on *Mulan, Lilo & Stitch, Emperor's New Groove, 101 Dalmatians, Crimson Tide, Terminal Velocity, Taking Care of Business,* and *Straight Talk*. As a screenwriter, he helped pen more than twenty feature screenplays for Paramount, Disney, DreamWorks, Fox, and Universal, including *Vampire In Brooklyn, Home On The Range, Good Intentions,* and *Spirit: Stallion of the Cimarron,* which was nominated for an Academy Award in 2002 as best animated feature. He is the author of *Crash! Boom! Bang! How to Write Action Movies*.

Ellen Malphrus is author of *Untying the Moon* (foreword by Pat Conroy). Her poetry and prose have been published in journals and collections including *Chariton; Weber: The Contemporary West; Poetry South; James Dickey Review; Blue Mountain Review; Natural Bridge; Southern Literary Journal; William & Mary Review; Fall Lines; Yemassee; Haight Ashbury Review; Catalyst; Without Halos;* and *Our Prince of Scribes.* She is Writer-in-Residence at USC Beaufort and divides her time between the rivers of her native South Carolina Lowcountry and mountains of western Montana. James Dickey was her teacher, mentor, and friend.

James Mann earned his Ph.D. in 1975 with James Dickey as his dissertation director. His meticulous notes from Dickey's classes are being serially excerpted by the *JDR.* In 2016, he published both *Tombstone Confidential,* consisting of 10,000 lines of rhymed pentameter quatrains, and *Manifesto of Vandalism,* a work of art theory. After years of university teaching, he served for a decade as Curator of the Las Vegas Art Museum.

Joyce Maynard first published her stories in magazines at age thirteen but was brought to the national spotlight in 1972 with her cover story in the *New York Times,* "An Eighteen Year Old Looks Back on Life." Donning the cover, she states, "My life was never the same." The author of eighteen books, including her recent novel, *Count the Ways,* she has worked as a reporter, a columnist, and a regular contributor to *NPR.* She also published in *Vogue* and *The New York Times Magazine.* Since 2001, she has conducted a week-long workshop on the art and craft of memoir at Lake Atitlan, Guatemala, where she founded Write by the Lake. Among her many publications, she is the author of *To Die For, Under the Influence, At Home in the World, The Best of Us,* as well as the New York Times bestselling novel, *Labor Day.*

Gloria Mindock is the author of *Ash* (Glass Lyre Press), *I Wish Francisco Franco Would Love Me* (Nixes Mate Books), *Whiteness of Bone* (Glass Lyre Press), *La Portile Raiului*, translated into Romanian by Flavia Cosma (Ars Longa Press, Romania), *Nothing Divine Here* (U Šoku Štampa, Montenegro), and *Blood Soaked Dresses* (Ibbetson St. Press). Widely published in the USA and abroad, her poetry has been translated and published into eleven languages. Gloria is editor of Červená Barva Press and was the Poet Laureate in Somerville, MA in 2017 and 2018. Her book *Ash* was awarded the Speak Up Talk Radio Firebird Book Award in July 2021. *Ash* is also translated into Serbian by Milutin Durickovic and will be out shortly by ALMA Press in Belgrade.

Nick Norwood's poems have appeared in *The Paris Review, Southwest Review, Western Humanities Review, Shenandoah, Poetry Daily, The Oxford American,* the PBS NewsHour site "Art Beat," U.S. Poet Laureate Ted Kooser's syndicated column "American Life in Poetry," NPR's "Writer's Almanac" with Garrison Keillor, and elsewhere. His four books are *Eagle & Phenix, Gravel and Hawk, A Palace for the Heart,* and *The Soft Blare.* He has been awarded a Pushcart Prize, the Hollis Summers Prize, and others.

Clayton H. Ramsey is a former two-term president of the Atlanta Writers Club, a 107-year-old, 1,000-member community of writers in the area, and currently serves as Officer Emeritus and Director of the AWC Townsend Prize for Fiction. A regular contributor to *Georgia Backroads* magazine, he has also been published in *The Writer, The Chattahoochee Review, The Blue Mountain Review,* and elsewhere. An Atlanta native, he has degrees from Princeton and Emory, has appeared on Georgia Public Broadcasting and National Public Radio, and has been honored for his work by *The Writer,* the Georgia Writers Museum, and the Atlanta Writers Club. He published *Viral Literature: Alone Together in Georgia*, an anthology of stories and poems related to the pandemic from 32 of the best writers in Georgia, in December 2020. He is married and lives in Decatur.

CONTRIBUTORS

Charlie Riccardelli lives in Denton, Texas. He earned his Ph.D. in English from the University of North Texas, where he teaches in the Department of Technical Communication. In addition, he works as an operations communications specialist for 7-Eleven Corporate. He has published essays, short stories, and reviews for *The American Literary Review, PopMatters, Hobart, Circa,* and *The Copperfield Review,* among others.

Jerry Rumph is a poet in Reinhardt's MFA program. He is currently studying many poets, including Lyn Hejinian, Larry Levis, James Wright, and Todd Davis, to name just a few. Jerry is interested in looking at the impact of institutional violence on marginalized voices and how those voices reclaim space in society. When not reading or writing literature, Jerry can be found spending time with his family, playing chess, and when he's really lucky, taking a long walk on the beach.

Jon Sokol is a writer, forester, traveler, and outdoorsman. He lives in Northeast Georgia with his wife, Karen. He mostly writes fiction, often drifting toward southern gothic and his fascination with all things peculiar. Jon's work has appeared in *Cowboy Jamboree, Gutwrench Journal, The Dead Mule School of Southern Literature,* and other journals and anthologies. In 2021, he graduated from Reinhardt University with an MFA in Creative Writing.

Carey Scott Wilkerson is a poet, dramatist, and opera librettist. His most recent works include a collection of the poetry, *Cruel Fever of the Sky,* a libretti for *The Heart is a Lonely Hunter,* an opera based on the classic Carson McCullers novel, and *The Rescue,* an operatic retelling of the Orpheus myth. He is an Assistant Professor of Creative Writing at Columbus State University and is currently working on a portrait opera about the famous African-American abstract expressionist painter, Alma Thomas (1891-1978).

You Will Be

A Writer in the New South

1883 **Reinhardt University**

ETOWAH VALLEY WRITING PROGRAM

Master of Fine Arts in Creative Writing

Earn Your Degree from Home
10-Day Summer Residency
Award-winning Writing Faculty

Made in United States
Orlando, FL
31 December 2021

12684072R00129